Y0-DDS-233

THIS ANGRY, LOVING LAND

THIS ANGRY, LOVING LAND

JEAN LENORE KENNY

BETHANY HOUSE PUBLISHERS
Minneapolis, Minnesota 55438
A Division of Bethany Fellowship, Inc.

Copyright © 1981
Jean Lenore Kenny
All rights reserved

Published by Bethany House Publishers
A division of Bethany Fellowship, Inc.
6820 Auto Club Road, Minneapolis, Minnesota 55438

Printed in the United States of America

Library of Congress Cataloging in Publication Data

Kenny, Jean Lenore, 1929-
   This angry, loving land.

   I. Title.
PS3556.R389T4   813'.54   81-10245
ISBN 0-87123-568-4 (pbk.)   AACR2

To my precious children,
for the years of your childhood.

O God, our God, . . . we have no strength to face this great horde which is invading our land; we know not what we ought to do; we lift our eyes to thee.

2 Chron. 20:12, NEB

To my precious children,
for the years of your childhood.

O God, our God, . . . we have no strength to face this great horde
which is invading our land; we know not what we ought to do; we
lift our eyes to thee.

2 Chron. 20:12, NEB

About the Author

JEAN LENORE KENNY was born in Eastern Montana. She is the wife of a pastor and the mother of four children. She has written several short stories and articles for publication. She has been very active in community work as a volunteer helper with retarded children. The author and her husband presently live at Lake View Bible Chapel, Hope, Idaho.

About the Author

JEAN LENORE KENNY was born in Eastern Montana. She is the wife of a pastor and the mother of four children. She has written several short stories and articles for publication. She has been very active in community work as a volunteer helper with retarded children. The author and her husband presently live at Lake View Bible Chapel, Hope, Idaho.

Contents

Prologue

Long ago most of the lights went out on the Montana prairie.
A dry wind huffed here and there; one by one the lanterns flick-
ered and died and darkness crept across the miles of rolling land.
Often there was nothing, not even a marker, to show where the
settlers and many small farmers had buried their youth before
they rode out and away, their heads bowed over humped shoulders, their eyes reflecting the emptiness of dead dreams. Only
the wind stayed behind, winnowing across the endless grass and
wheatlands like Rachael mourning for her children. Co-ome ho-
ome, the wind moaned, chh-ill-un', co-ome ho-ome.

So when a community of religious fanatics rode the back of a
chinook breeze into Ordlow County in an early spring of the late
1970s, it was the observation of field hand John Johnson that the
children were coming back to the prairie.

They came with matted bedrolls and blackened kettles and
garden seeds and worn Bibles. They came with hearts heavy
from the solemn trumpets of coming judgment, from the clanking chains of back streets and ghettos, from churches that cooed
at their new sainthood and clucked at their awful visions and
even worse clothing. They came like lepers seeking their own cat-
acombs.

They settled on forty acres belonging to John Johnson. The
acreage boasted a rambling barn, a battered toolshed and a forgotten schoolhouse. Some of them lived in the barn that was so
old it listed east and south and shuddered in the wind. The rest
of them lived in the schoolhouse where the pioneers before them
had learned to read and write.

After the chinook had sent the last mound of dirty snow into a
murky stream, they plowed up a field for their garden. Carefully
they planted corn and peas and beans and carrots and seed potatoes. In late spring they set out tomato plants. They bought a
bum lamb and a calf and fenced off a grazing spot for them.

All season long they coaxed and nursed the sod for their bread. It was a harsh land, harsh and dry. In July the water level in the well sank so low that only a thin, muddy trickle belched from the pump. With struggling patience the fanatics carted water in old cans placed carefully in the trunks of their rattling cars. From rain barrels stashed under crumbling eaves of the buildings, from the distant river, from the park spigot in town, they faithfully watered their vegetables. They hoed weeds vigorously and brushed the beetles away with swift, angry fingers.

In order to get into the town of Ordlow from the west, you had to pass right by the commune. The feelings among hard-working, efficient farmers and business folk in that area ranged from curiosity to suspicion to hostility; and it was said in Ordlow that these young folks used dope and practiced some sort of witchcraft, that they were possessed by bad spirits, that they lived like pigs and, that more of their kind were flocking in every day. It was said that they would soon be begging welfare funds, sponging off the tax money produced by hard-working, honest people. It was said that something must be done.

The clamor for action became so loud it drowned the lonesome, plaintive cry of John Johnson who warned them to "let the babies alone." Everyone knew that Johnson was a fool and the world was getting to be more of a hellhole every minute and it was the young generation's fault; there just weren't enough true sons of the prairie like their own young Kettrie brothers to hold the world steady much longer.

1

Going On

Those summer years cry to be awakened,
leave them be, love is not forsakened;
the storehouse of winter is full.[1]

IT WAS LATE NIGHT when Urliss Peterson arrived at Shellydown ranch from her home in Norway. But in spite of the darkness, she could sense the land out there, the American Prairie, silent and listening, yet muttering all at once and going on forever. It was the swelling dawn which brought with it an eagle falling from the big sky, falling to a field that was dark and waiting, fresh ripped by plow. Then the haze lifted; the sun spilled over the edge of the field and she saw how it all went from spinning gold to umber. She heard the sounds of the land, the gulls screeching, the cattle bellowing through the coulees, and the great sea of insects lisping at the sod. But then, when the morning was ripe the wind started in, tearing and groaning. It frightened her, all of it, the land with its stark endless expanse and the hungry wind that tore away at it. But even more disturbing was the anger she felt toward her uncle's long-ago friend, Dow Garstin, who had met her at the airport and brought her to this wilderness.

It was that anger, all bound up with the lingering impression of the man whom she had met for the first time at the busy terminal last night, that had kept her from sleep, kept her jumping from bed to window where she paced a dozen steps across the floor and repeated it all over again through the hours of dark and dawn and morning. "A brute he be," she whispered for the twentieth time, "and de reason I feel lifeless as a blob."

His very presence had cowed her, exuding as he did such in-

---

1. From "Summer Years" by J. Kenny. All poetry written by the author.

tense pride and power. Her tongue, anxious for more practice in the unfamiliar language, had been stilled and her hands left to fist and flutter like trembling birds in their cages. From uneasiness to defensive resentment and back again, she had struggled for some common ground on which to shatter his silent indifference to her company. Because he had ignored her, all through the long ride to the ranch, treating her like a block of wood instead of a sensitive woman who had been an honored member of her community back among the salty coves of her Atlantic village.

Only those desperate days of World War II could have drawn her kindly uncle to the side of such a rude, arrogant man. Her thoughts hammered away at him, slipping back into her mother tongue. It was hard to imagine how their bond of friendship had been so intimately forged that after all these years her uncle could request Mr. Garstin to help her get settled in America. The cattle baron had responded with a plea of his own, that Urliss come to Ordlow County for a little while to help with the caring of two young fellows, neighbors of Dow's, recently bereaved of their parents. She had rushed about for two weeks as she secured her papers and tickets, and packed. So here she was, far from the glamorous American cities and the crowded beaches, far from her opportunity to find a good, rich Lutheran who could cherish her with a sailing boat and a cliff house over the ocean "till death do us part."

"I vill not stay here long," she vowed aloud to the sun that was trying to melt her into the cellar through the long, skinny window of her assigned bedroom. With eyes dry and smarting, she continued to peer out at the big yard with its arched gateway over a path leading to a straggling barn and stable in the distance. Even as she watched, with lanky strides two young men came into view directly below her.

So these are the Kettrie brothers, she thought, recalling bitterly that Mr. Garstin had told her nothing about them except that they would be attending their parents' memorial service this afternoon. They were dressed in light shirts and slacks that flapped against their legs in the gusting wind. "Poor *foreldreløse*, poor orphans," she murmured, examining them with sympathetic interest, her anger at Dow momentarily forgotten.

One of them turned and looked up at her. Their gaze locked for a moment and she caught the solemn sadness hanging about his slender frame like a distilled aura. She was stirred by a sort of wistful longing, a pleasant feeling that made her feel less a stranger. When he turned away, she went over to the mirror and smoothed her hair.

Like the ranges out there, she was tawny gold from crown to heel, her eyes deep blue and rimmed now with tired creases. "A beautiful, pure lady, that one," her brothers had often boasted, explaining away her vitriolic disposition by putting the blame on seizures of colitis and brain fever early in her life.

But no amount of explaining had coaxed any but the most spirited young men to the front door of her Norwegian home; a fine dilemma it was for the proud, romance-loving Urliss who privately despaired of ever attracting a good husband, even though she was outwardly scornful, pretending she had no use for any man. None of them was good enough for her. Her brothers knew that. But yet they grudgingly agreed with their sympathetic uncle that a journey to America, where her choleric outbursts might be better tolerated in her pursuit of the proper mate, would be a wise sacrifice for them all. She had thirty-five years on her now. It was time she be settled away for a while. So they committed her to the care of the *Herre Gud*, Lord God, and sent her off with reminders that she could return to them anytime, and either Olin or Gar, their bachelor friends, would be highly honored to take her to wife. "I vill die before I be a vife to eider of dose two!" she had seethed between trembling, outraged lips, though with enough presence of mind to practice her English. She had resolutely bade farewell to home, family, and set her mind to even think in the foreign tongue.

But now she had to put all thoughts of home and family again to rest beneath the plaintive call of that young Kettrie boy in the courtyard who had seemed to pipe to her from his spirit. She would get acquainted with the kitchen, and then she would make some lunch and call the brothers to eat. "I be de only girl in a big family back in Norvay," she would tell them. "Ah, yah, I am used to good men; now tell me how it be vid you? Let us be friends."

That afternoon a white sun scorched the grass around the new graves in the Ordlow cemetery so that it lay limp and bleached, exposing the pale clumps of earth, creased and scarred from the harvest drought that raced like a lean hound across the prairie. The mourners squinted against the unveiled sky and shuffled the hot, heavy weight of their bodies as they flicked a quick gaze at the bereaved Kettrie boys, poised like bronzed spears at the edge of the pits.

College-bound Ethan, older by eleven months, was a shade shorter and huskier than his brother. Sweat clung to the wedge above his lip like tiny blisters, and gusts of wind ruffled his hair into little brass shags. He sensed his brother's grief melding with his own. He turned and stared at Kip and their eyes locked, revealing their love for each other, strong and familiar, like two saplings grown from the same roots. Thank God Almighty we're together, their eyes said. Together they gave off a haunting energy that fell like a requiem across the ceremony.

Behind the brothers their father's friend, Dow Garstin, dwarfed the crowd, his unspoken reproach as heavy as the thunder that rolled against the sullen cloud bank in the far west. Dow had never approved of Ed Kettrie's race-horse fevers, or his flights to world-renowned tracks; and now this obsession had ended up costing Ed and Ila their lives. Next to him the long frame of John Johnson, Kettrie's hired hand, stood politely in a little dip of earth. He had given years of devoted service, driving old tractors around the fields, welding them together with scrap iron when they came unglued, then going back at it, around the fields again until it was time to cut wheat or bind the oats or ride leather to fall pasture.

And now the little band of mourners were filing away. Some of them would find a cool tavern where they could soothe their dry, swollen tongues and pick at their memories.

As the mourners went off to reminisce in tears or levity, no one intruded on the brothers by pumping their arms and muttering condolences. Ethan was thankful for that. While John Johnson stood by, his head bowed respectfully over his chest, Ethan and Kip waited, waited until the soft ploddings of retreating footsteps and muffled door slams and purring cars had faded away. Silently they stood beside the caskets while the wind shuffled like crippled feet through the brittle grass and little trails and hollows of the cemetery.

When Ethan spoke it was with the edge of a long-suppressed diatribe. "Wonder why your big ol' God did this, John," he accused bitterly. "Wonder how long they lay there alive after the crash, their flesh fallin' away, the three weeks it took to find them? Our sweet mama and good-hearted daddy—wonder what sort of a God would treat them this way? They were always kind to you, weren't they?" A tiny vein above his eye charged to and fro convulsively.

John shook his head sadly. "Son—" he pleaded.

With controlled rage Ethan turned on him. "I'm no son of yours; we've nothin' together, you and me! You're always mumblin' to the Big Boy up there for your ki-yi buddies off the reservation. But you musta' forgot to pray for our folks! Well, never mind, I never believed for a minute that you had any influence with Him anyhow!"

"There now, Ethan, they're in God's hands."

"That's s'posed to comfort us? Your God is my nightmare!" He lowered his voice so that it sounded old and dry, like sticks rubbing together. "Know where they really are, John? They're ashes in the grainfields, the same fields my dad worked and sweated over. Fertilizer for our Wheaties—that's what we're all gonna be, you and that bunch of loonies camped over on your land included. That's how we're all gonna end up, no more hurtin' and bleedin', just ashes and compost for the weeds and barley."

Misery crowded John's dark eyes as he slowly shook his head. Ethan rasped on, "Know what I think of your God, John?" He slammed a taut fist at the sky and swore.

Kips's mouth trembled with the effort of speech. "You're crazy, Ethan; now cut it out!" Fear of his brother's sudden madness folded into his own anguish so that he could feel his heart give way, feel it oozing through his pores, feel it gliding down his torso, over his legs and onto his feet, wrapping them in throbbing chains.

Ethan turned on him. "You're a baby!" he raved, "complainin' and whimperin'!"

"I n-never did cry—wish I could," Kip stammered, his face working with distress.

"We'll see to it you get your brownie button for that stiff lip, little brother." His eyes glinted with unnatural light. Suddenly he lunged, tackling his brother around the knees. "Let's see if you can make *me* cry!"

They wrestled then, gasping and grunting and hurting themselves for all the grief that clung around their chests, poking and tearing at their feelings the way they used to work the springs through the fiber of their old mohair sofa by jumping up and down on it. After a while they lay in the dust, sobbing and wet and retching and rolling over with eyes closed against the jagged spurs of sun, their breath groaning out and away. They lay inert. Distant echoes of children calling fell across the new stillness.

The sun started down. Mosquitoes roused from the shade of the grass, droning their hunger. John turned away from his sentry duty by the new graves. "Get up now, boys," he said in a thin, sad voice. He went back to his own truck and headed for the harvest fields.

Ethan crawled to his feet. "Give me your hand, little brother," he said softly. Kip lifted his arm and let Ethan help him up; they went limping and shuffling away to the pickup and started home.

Home was a sea of wheat twenty miles north of town, a herd of cows flung like red ants across the rolling hills. They drove through town and past fields where combines chewed and spit grain like a regiment of grasshoppers, past the commune of religious fanatics which they refused to acknowledge with the turn of their heads. "Leeches," Ethan muttered automatically.

The commune was a bitter reminder that the great prairie was slowly being prostituted by outsiders, by recreation developers and sidewalk land grabbers who sat in their distant city offices and waited for a rush to this last frontier so they could greedily fill their pockets from an inflated market. And now these rootless hippies were moving in, looking for an outpost where they could degenerate without intrusion.

The whole world has turned sour, Ethan decided. Nothing

was right anymore, particularly not his brother who was now all folded into himself, looking even more pathetic and forlorn under the fresh scars of their skirmish. Pity for him turned his stomach to lead. "Poor boy," he muttered, "you've never been anywhere, never seen anything, and now you'll be alone." Ethan looked at Kip. "Maybe I should wait a year for college, stay at home so we can work things out together."

"Quit babyin' me," he said.

"The folks always did."

"Well, I'm a big boy now."

Ethan grunted and gave him a hard look. "With Dow Garstin callin' the turns, you'll grow up fast, you can bet on it." He thought about that for a minute and when he spoke again he slurred his thoughts through his tongue in jarring monosyllables. "Wonder why the folks left him in charge of everything, even us—as if we needed him."

"They were friends, and Dow's smart."

Ethan said, the anger creeping back into his voice, "Think you can hold your own with him?"

"I've always respected him," Kip said.

"I respect him, too," Ethan murmured, "like I respect a rattlesnake."

"Don't grouse at me about it," Kip said mildly. His features, regular and even, almost beautiful, were suffused with the light of the dying sun.

"No sense in it," Ethan agreed. "You'll find out quick enough that Dow's a smart operator—for himself, that is. I know what I want and I'm goin' after it; but you—" he shrugged and shook his head helplessly, "you don't know much of anything." His stomach growled fitfully. "We're late for dinner; that means the mermaid has scorched the potatoes. 'Vat you guys tink? I haf nodding to do but keep de spuds varm?' " Kip grinned at his brother's exaggerated imitation of the lady from Norway, the sudden humor half covering the listless, sad look of him. Already Urliss was taking over the house as if she had built it, but there was some comfort in having her around.

They arrived home to symphonies rising from the sloughs and gullies, anthems of crickets and frogs bleating their eulogy at the red flare of sun falling behind the hills. For a minute they sat in the rig and looked out the window at the ghosts of their parents weaving in and out of the house and drifting across the meadows and hallooing through the barnyard. "Nothing will ever be the same," Ethan said, Kip nodding slowly.

When they went inside Urliss regarded their disheveled appearance with curiosity and horror, her expression conveying that she was even now suspecting the sanity of her role as mother-protector to the likes of them both. "You vas in a fight, no doubt!" She shooed them toward peroxide and bandages while stirring vigorously the thrice-warmed gravy and roast beef, bustling dutifully from cupboard to stove to table. The dimple in her chin set off a whole colony of little dimples as her face reflected the range of her feelings. "Now explain, explain!" she called after them until she heard the bath water running. Her face flushed with uneasiness. "Cranky boys," she muttered.

Later, while Ethan and Kip gobbled up their food, Urliss went to the screen door and looked out at the harvest moon coming up big and amber and low over the dark knoll, tilting her ear to the land rumbling and teeming with life. Watching her drooping shoulder in the doorway, Kip felt her loneliness and was sorry for her. When she turned he caught her eye and gave her a quick smile—he was drawn to her in ways he could not define. "You're a good cook, Urliss," he said, "and it's great to feel hungry."

Urliss flushed with sudden pleasure. After a bit she drew up a chair beside them. "Now, den, vat happen?" She looked from one to the other with genuine concern.

Over the rim of his cup Ethan peered at her thoughtfully. She was a handsome, full-blown woman with a generous mouth and a little cleft in her lower lip. He picked up his fork again before answering. "We were ambushed," he explained between mouthfuls. "It happened on the north fork comin' home. There was this carload of Norwegians out lookin' t'make trouble for landed gentry like us; they outnumbered us two to one."

Urliss blinked confusion. "Dey yust vant to fight? Dey say notting?"

"Oh, yeah, they called us some names and demanded our silver dollars. But we gave 'em a good run, didn't we, Kip? They went off in worse shape than we are. And we learned somethin' "
—he paused, frowning—"Norwegians are all mouth and no mus-

cle."

It was plain Urliss could not decide whether his story had any merit, but an angry flush swelled across her face. She got up proudly, taking her glass to the sink. Her words fell like ice cubes in a tin bucket. "I go now to bed. You clean up dis mess, do de dishes." She moved stiffly down the hall.

Kip said, pushing back his chair and getting up, "You make me sick," in a mild tone.

"She can't take a joke."

"She can hardly speak the language, let alone understand your dumb jokes. She has feelings, though."

"So do I." He wolfed the rest of his food. "She's a brain picker—has to know everything. I have feelings about that." He dished up a bowl of cobbler. "I'll dry the plates," he promised, but he dawdled until Kip had washed them in a mountain of suds and then he said, "Let 'em air awhile," and went outdoors. Kip followed him.

Dusk was filtering in, blurring the outline of the rambling barn and graneries. The brothers shuffled to the corral and climbed the haystack where they lay like partly opened jack-knives in the scooped-out place on top and watched the sky fill up with spangled bracelets. It seemed that the stars in the sky and the town far away and the whole world knew their sorrow and grieved right along with them. "Some ways I'm glad to be going away," Ethan said, "but I'll miss you, Kip. I worry about you, ya' dumb kid."

"I'll get along. Just don't forget me when you're famous."

"I'm gonna be the best lawyer on the western scene, but I won't forget you, little brother. After a year with Dow you'll probably need me."

They fell silent for a while. Kip spoke again, "I keep thinking that any minute the screen door's going to slam and Dad's going to beller at us from the stoop, 'All field hands to bed now!' " He could see his brother's face go soft, his brows slouching over his eyes.

"Yeah, they sure feel close, don't they?"

They heard a car and watched for it on the road. When the headlights whirled into their lane, Ethan mumbled, "Ol' deliberate Dowlie."

Kip whistled through his teeth. Dow Garstin wasn't the type of man you made fun of. In his defense he said, "He drives himself hard."

"He drives everyone up the windmill."

They stayed glued to the stack, concentrating on the car that was being trailed now by a combine. Dow drove into the yard and parked. When the combine drew alongside, he stepped out and hailed the driver. "Come down, John!" he ordered sharply.

John turned off the motor and jumped to the ground. Even in the dark the brothers knew from familiar exposure just how John looked with layers of grain dust masking the clawed-out furrows of his face, even after only a couple hours' work in the harvest.

Dow lit his pipe and sucked on it. "John, you're tired and it's been a long day. But we have a problem." He blew smoke and drew closer to him. "It's that bunch of kids you've got camped on your forty out of Ordlow. Guess you know they're not very popular."

John took off his cap and brushed at his forehead. "Yessir," he chuckled, "I hear the city fathers are up in arms over those children; that's both funny and sad, Dow."

"Maybe. Maybe not. They think the commune affects the health of the town, John. They don't want that hippie element hanging around. People in this county have worked hard to raise wholesome children, and they don't want them ruined by bad company, you know that."

"I don't mean to sound bull-headed, Dow," John said pleasantly, "but you can tell them for me that these children are harmless; they're a community of Christians; they wanted a place where they could live simply, garden a bit, that sort of thing. I've gotten acquainted with their leader, Ben Rutledge; he lived in the Dakotas as a boy, loves the plains, says they're medicine to the messed-up kids he's helping."

"Medicine, eh? Now how do they propose to survive to take their medicine, living off forty acres of dry land? You know they can't, John, or you would have worked it yourself. They'll be starvin' and thievin' in our backyards, and you know it!"

John went on doggedly, "You're right, they can't live off that piece of sod. But they're willing to work—grew a nice bunch of corn and potatoes; they're not loafers, and they've been taking jobs where they can find them. How about giving them a chance? If the elements and the dry land 're too much for them, they'll move on without any persuasion from us."

Dow's voice grew edgy. "Half the town swears that they have friends coming here on dope. You'll have to get them out."

"Those kids are all right," John repeated stubbornly. "They're not bothering anyone. It'll soon be winter, and one of their women has a new baby. I can't send them out."

"Then the responsibility will have to fall to others."

"Listen, Dow, this prairie is like an old mama with a big lap. There's room here for a whole world of people. Why, the plains are lonesome for young blood."

"You're a fool, Johnson," Dow said quietly. "You give yourself airs as champion of the weak. But what about the strong, John? The strong man sweats blood so you can spin your fables and play Robin Hood for the grandstand; it's as simple as that."

"You braggin' again, Dow?" John teased without malice. He hoisted himself back onto the combine. "Take it easy." He gave a brisk salute and put the machine into motion once more.

"Old fool," Dow muttered, striking out for the house. The two boys watched him go until Kip gave Ethan a poke.

"Hey there, Dow!" Ethan called.

Dow turned and stopped short when he spied the brothers appearing from the shadow of the haystack. "Boys," he called out, "everything all right?"

"Fine, fine," Ethan said.

"How're you getting along with Urliss?"

"As long as her cookin' holds up we'll survive," Kip answered.

"Well, I'm on my way home; just thought I'd check on you." He paused as if he would speak again, turned around and went swiftly back to his car.

As they watched him leave, Ethan growled, "I don't blame him for getting uptight about John's misfits. As long as I've know that half-breed, he's been tending a lot of bums." He catapulted over a stray bale of hay. "And championing a bunch of retards raising wormy tomatoes makes me even more suspicious of John." He set out for the house.

Kip stood looking at the bunkhouse where a dim light shone through the window. He remembered the day of John's arrival at

Shellydown because Kip had just returned home from his first day of school, colliding with him at the back door where he had loomed like a lonely rover looking for a home.

"He's a good man," their father would say many times as the years chipped away at John's physical strength, "tender as a nurse; but he's got no sense about folks, thinks they're all as decent as he is." But John's capacity for hard, conscientious work became legendary throughout the county so that he grew acceptable to the proud, independent ranchers in spite of the fact that he entertained all shades of company, most of it questionable.

When Kip finally reached the upstairs landing, he was so preoccupied with his thoughts that he had to take a second look out the window before the realization of something out there registered in his mind. Even as he watched, a glow on the southern horizon grew taller and became a dancing flame. Quickly he bolted into Ethan's room where his brother lay spread-eagled on the bed with the fan turned on him. "Looks like fire at Martin's!" he yelled. "I'll go ahead; you fill the tank with water and follow!" Without giving him a chance for a retort, he dashed back down the steps and into the pickup, tearing out of the driveway and down the lane.

In no time Kip saw that the fire had become a billowing spire and that it was not Martin's place after all but farther south. A fire in harvest was the nemesis of every grower; it could sweep like wind over tender dry grain and grasslands, snuffing the life out of them.

At the highway he turned toward Ordlow, and it was only moments until he saw that it was the old, rambling barn on John's acreage that was ablaze.

When he drew up the yard was alive with bystanders who were doing little but standing around looking on; but the outlying fields were dotted with private weed-spray rigs used to scatter water where burning fagots were being hurled like torches from the blazing building. Someone said that they had called for the fire truck, and it should be here any minute. There was nothing for Kip to do but join the bystanders and stare as the skeletal frame of the great building heaved, shuddered and crashed to the ground as if it were falling into hell's chambers.

Beside him a woman wept softly. Kip turned to look at her

and then at the others who formed a cluster of sad, stern faces, pale even in the brilliant light. The men were bearded and the women were dressed in cotton prints that fell to their ankles. While most of them stared softly ahead, two of the women had their eyes shut and their lips moved silently.

Kip felt annoyed. It's only an old barn, he wanted to tell them, not as if someone was hurt. If they had stood by their parents' graves as he had this afternoon, then they would have cause to grieve, he thought bitterly. He remembered that these young people had chosen to leave parents and homes, that they were bums and rebels with no feeling for anyone but themselves. They had no business being here at all; they should go back where they belonged. Their carelessness in burning the old barn had endangered the fields of everyone around.

The fire truck never did make an appearance. Long after the flames had died to sporadic, licking tongues in the smoldering heap, the women at Kip's elbow continued to pray. Kip felt someone's eyes on him and turned around to stare back at the saddest, tenderest face he had ever seen. The girl, likely no older than he was and with dark hair falling to her waist, was not pretty but had such poignancy stamped into her face that Kip froze and said tightly, "Howdy," with a quick little nod before going off to his pickup. Thoughtfully he peered through the windshield at the forlorn girl, feeling strangely sad and angry. It had been a rotten day all through, and he would wait till morning to tell John that his barn was gone.

2

The Game

He hurts, my hurting boy.
For him let me touch your throne,
In my sackcloth of shredded pride,
In ashes of contrition, myself denied,
Take my sweets and wine. . . .

WITH RUSTLING SKIRTS and late dew that settled everywhere like iced teardrops, autumn came to the prairie. Long tails of smoke trailed from chimneys in early morning, and the wind died down and stillness hung like an old coat over the rain barrel.

The children went back to school. The farmers camped around their machine sheds and emptied their grease guns on cranky equipment. Then they charged into town where they talked shop and listened to the stock and grain reports, drank fountains of coffee and sat in the hotel lobby and waited. Waited for a neighbor to finish shopping, waited for school to let out. Their wives slept until the sun was warm through the windows, and then they got out their sewing machines and stitched a new dress and stared idly into space. There was a great deal of movement and inertia—movement getting ready for winter and friendly socials, inertia from letting down after the long work season.

Dow Garstin drove his truck through the big pastures, counting cows and examining fences. He parked finally at the foot of a knoll, turned off the ignition and got out of the cab. As he started up the hill he sucked in great gulps of the biting air until drunk with it, looking around at the land sweeping away to distance-dimmed hills. West and south he owned it all as far as the eye could see. Over the years he had swallowed up his neighbors one by one, watching them move out and away, their strength surrendered to the dust clouds rolling in from the breeches and to the wind howling its savage melancholy through field and home, into the beams and gullies of their souls. Good-bye, Murphys. Good-bye, Smiths. Good-bye, Javers. Now good-bye, Kettries.

It pained him to finish the ill-fated chore of tearing the Kettrie boys' lives apart; but he must make them understand that he could hold the ranch together for one more year, until Kip left for college, and then the mortgage would have to be met, the outstanding bills paid. There would be precious little left.

When the boys grew older they would realize that their father, that amiable, fun-loving man, had bled his land to finance his horse-racing obsessions with Kentucky blue stock and travels that took him and Ila around the world, the track in South America giving them the last good time and costing them their lives.

The boys were good-looking, bright, personable. They would get along all right.

Yes, they would get along, Dow thought. There would be enough money from the sale of the land to educate them and give them a good start. Ethan wanted to be a lawyer; there was money there for a good man. And Kip? What would he do? Teach, maybe. He was a pleasant lad, not exactly forceful but warm and kind-hearted. He looked like his mother, had her ways.

His mother. Ila. The thought of her made Dow's mouth tighten with little creases of pain and his eyes mellow with an old grief. A man who had always kept his own counsel, the love he had known for Ila had been concealed even from her. Because he was a gentleman and Ed Kettrie had been his friend, Dow had maintained his reserve in both distance and speech whenever Ila was present or whenever he had been a guest in the Kettrie home; but as far back as he could remember she had come unbidden to his thoughts on wings of inexpressive longing, so that now her death held out a mocking sort of promise, and he wondered at the feeling of loss for something that had never belonged to him. At least, he thought grimly, at least it was final now. Over.

Yes—he brought himself back—Ila's boys had a lot going for them; they would get along fine. Dow's lips parted and his eyes peered sadly ahead of himself. He thought of his own boyhood and the swollen, polluted city far away and groaned softly, because he knew that the Kettrie loins were full of prairie, and every time the sun squatted like raw fire in the west or the northern lights charged eerily across the sky or an eagle took wing like a new kite tossing, the boys would think of home, and they would shrivel up inside like old men dying.

His boots sloughed dust from the grass as he went back to the truck, his thoughts tumbling within. He well knew the correct formula for life; he knew it in the habit of his own practice, that it should be lived with one's mind, will, and emotions all groomed to that excellent code of patriarch and nobleman, disciplined to sacrifice at the altar of wisdom and character. But there were times even now when the struggle erupting midway between the poles of responsibility and devilish rebellion kicked little chinks into the iron of his resolve and broke through the pores of his wind-whipped skin like acid cankers.

He jerked gears and wheeled on until he was nosing the Shellydown fence. Up creek was a meadow where someone should have built a house long ago. He stared hard and snatched up his field glasses to stare again. What is that Norwegian woman doing this far from the house? he wondered as he put the glasses down and started moving again. She was a puzzle, that woman, as handsome as a maid on a billboard with a behavior as unexpected as her personality—shy at times, arrogant and blunt at other times, maybe undergoing some sort of identity crisis this far from her homeland. He got out, opened a gate and steered the rig over an elusive trail.

"Here, Pliny, kom!" Urliss called to the mongrel who had almost gained a rabbit which he was furiously chasing; she could not stand the sight of bloodshed or suffering, not even those bruised egos that were the result of her own furious tongue and temper; those crushed feelings must be repaired quickly or she would suffer undue remorse. No, she could not stand the sight of abuse, and if Pliny was only playing a game with the hare, he was succeeding in frightening the poor creature out of its wits.

The dog paid no heed to her shrieks. She picked up a stone and hurled it with rage, catching him on the hind quarter so that he broke into sharp yelping and increased his stride. He had soon passed the poor rabbit who continued running for dear life even after Pliny had hurtled ahead, giving in finally to a wide arc that led it into a clump of grass on a side hill. "Vill teach you, dom hund!" Urliss shouted at the animal who returned to her now, his head bowing by fits and starts over his drooping tongue. "Dumb dog," Urliss carefully muttered again thinking of Ethan's mirthful corrections of her Scandinavian brogue. She gave the dog a couple quick pats before dismissing him from her thoughts which were now being stalked by the memories of home and the disappointment of this barren hinterland.

Already her brothers were sending warm letters of encouragement, inquiring whether she had yet found her ideal mate and reminding her of bachelors Gar and Olin, still available, at home. While she tore those letters into tiny pieces over the ash can, her face grew twisted and moist. "Tank da Lord Gud dey cannot see me now," she whispered bitterly.

She was sure her brothers knew that her scheme to find happiness in America was contingent on getting discovered by a suitor of some means who would grant her a life by the ocean where they could yacht and fish and romp through the beaches. Instead here she was in this unfriendly wasteland, cast in the role of nursemaid to two bereaved boys who made unrealistic demands on her patience. Besides that, the men within her grasp gave her fits of self-pity and hysterical weeping—that visionary, John, with his extra-heartiness, and that terrifying rancher baron, Dow Garstin, who was responsible for bringing her so far from the romantic life she had envisioned.

A roaring motor shattered her reverie and she whirled around, frowning at the truck wobbling toward her until wariness gave in to recognition. "Speak of da devil." She tried out her new American slang. Then her strength fell away so that she caught her trembling hands together, begging her composure to return.

Over the raspy motor Dow called, "Saw you from my field. You're not having trouble?"

"No trouble, I come here sometime." Dow's steel gray eyes looking right through her and reducing her motives to those of a frivolous school girl, by effect if not by inference, had become the bane of her waking moments. She grew defensive in his presence, sounding like a crotchety old maid, a suggestion she was trying to squelch by assuming an air of controlled indifference.

"Can't blame you for that, one of the greener spots around."

His manner, as usual, was polite but impatient. "Like a ride?"

Unnerved by him, she hesitated, frozen into the sky and field, until he noisily shifted the gears of his truck and then she flung herself into the cab, leaving the dog to go home by himself. "De meadow is green, remind me of Norvay, green patches in de mountains," she explained nervously. "I valk trough de coulees and pick de vildflower sometime. And if de grainfield vas green, it remind me of de sea ven de vind blow, like de vaves rolling."

Dow gave her a quick look and smiled. "Nice."

Urliss could see that he was pleased. She, too, nodded and smiled, and then fell to wondering about him: he was strong and good-looking as a king; why was he not married? Did he have someone? It did not seem normal for such a man to be alone.

But the jerking, shuddering movement of the truck over the lumpy sod jiggled her around like a cup of half-set jello, bringing her to the conclusion that it had been rude of Dow to ask her to ride in this dusty rig. This showed how little regard he had for a real lady. As they lumbered through the grassland, Urliss's outrage mounted until it had shut the lid on her timid spirit. "Dis is a poor truck, like a hay vagon," she complained imperiously.

Dow grunted. "Won't be long till you're home," he said. A minute later he added, "Your English is very good."

"Norvay teach English in school, start vid fourt grade; long time ago now for Urliss."

"How're you getting along? You like the ranch, do you?"

"Vell, not too much, no. I like Kipper," she added.

"Good. And Ethan? You like him, too?"

"Oh, yah, he is cocky, but—"

"I'll talk to him."

"No, do not talk; soon he go avay to school. He is good."

Dow nodded. "He *is* a good boy; I think a little cynical for his age, but a good worker; nothing like either of his folks, though."

They rode in silence until the house sprawled before them. "I hear you're getting acquainted in town," Dow said.

Urliss's face grew soft with pleasure. "Yah, de town is good; I vould not mind to live dere."

"Glad to hear it." Dow smiled his approval as he pulled into the driveway. Urliss jumped out, murmuring thanks before she receded into the back entrance, feeling Dow's eyes on her until she had shut the door. Immediately she made up her mind to stop her shaking, to get herself under control and the rancher baron out of her mind. "He is big landowner, stole it all from poor folk and Indians at de beginning, you bet," she muttered to her trembling hands.

The kitchen was in turmoil with Kip's books scattered across the table and the cake which was to have been their dinner dessert a ramble of crumbs on the floor. "A mystery how dat boy stay so skinny," Urliss murmured, "bottomless pit dat he be." She took out the broom and dustpan and swept up the crumbs and then stared out the window, her eyes darting curiously for a glimpse of the boys. She was relieved to catch sight of them breaking through the corral gate. In a moment they would explode through the door and their voices would crash against the kitchen as they shared with each other the events of Kip's school day which had separated them from each other for the first time in eleven years. They talked about football almost constantly, and Urliss could sense that Ethan was the star player of that game, while Kip was striving to please him with mildly encouraging reports of his own performance.

Their dialogue pointed up the difference between them, Urliss thought, Ethan with his easy confidence and Kip, as fine-sensed as his limbs with their cat-like strength flowing from his broad shoulders. He called to her through little confusions and sad looks that were siphoned off from the dependence of his spirit, so that she devoted herself to him with the full intensity of her disappointed heart.

Tonight was to be Ordlow's first football game of the season, and Ethan had persuaded her and John to go and root for Kip; so Urliss had spent the morning getting ready for it, washing her hair and brushing it until it glistened like grain stubble when the sun hit it. She had even persuaded John to take her to town where she finally bought the fashionable leather boots and suede jacket which she had eyed with trepidation on earlier occasions, her first paycheck heavy in her handbag and the maiden in her, wistful to show off her beauty, even now shaking the dust from her old skirt and the solitude from her arms. "I vill cheer for Kip so he be de best player of all, my engel boy."

Ah, how proud the brothers would be of her tonight. She

could even now hear them telling their friends: "Yes, that great lady belongs to us; she is mermaid from the land of the midnight sun."

As she measured milk and sugar into a kettle for a romegrad to replace the dessert cake, she hummed under her breath snatches of songs from her native land.

For dinner Urliss had made a great stew, and she fussed over Kip with anxious eyes, insisting he stuff enough into his stomach to sink a performing quarterback. "Have more!" she commanded, even though he held up a restraining hand, rolling his eyes and rubbing his stomach. "Is wery good for football boy," she assured him, "so you vill play best game of all." Already she was trying out the unfamiliar but stylish boots, clomping strenuously from table to cupboard, beaming on "my men," but directing her pride toward Kip who was involved in something so important tonight that Ethan had talked of little else all week.

When the dishes were put away, she treated herself to clouds of warm, frothy suds that mushroomed over the top of the six-legged tub. Tilting her head back against the edge, she closed her eyes, blotting out all but this warm, soothing minute. Contentment came to her there, like a tabby lying in the sun, and for the first time since her arrival at Shellydown, a glad anticipation swept over her.

A door slammed and she raised herself from her reverie and the tub at the same time. Standing before the long, steamed-over mirror that blurred her reflection, womanly and golden as blowing pollen, she gave a short, sardonic laugh, thinking of herself and how the solitary life converged on her till her energies raced helplessly through her body. Her living sacrifice of towering, fretful hungers was kept pure in its prison year in and out, in obedience to the Lord God who commanded a Thou Shalt Not restraint until He sent a good Lutheran to cover her with his chaste and holy mantle.

Rubbing herself hard with a towel, she murmured, "Lord, if you do not send a good man to Urliss soon now, it vill be too late. Nobody vants an old maid."

Later, as she rode in Ethan's car to the game in Ordlow, Urliss kept up a steady stream of chatter, overpowering both Ethan and John Johnson who kept nodding and smiling from the back-seat where he hunched into his frayed mackinaw. "Vas good of you, Etan, to ask me to de game," she said pleasantly, hoping Ethan would respond that it was good of her to show this interest.

"Glad you're coming, Urliss," he returned. "Man, I hope Kip's not too nervous," he added, fidgeting while he drove and betraying his own nervousness.

"Vy, I am glad to do it; you boys interest me wery much!" She turned, smiling on John. "I get lonely for my brudders in Norvay. Kip and Etan, dey are my little American brudders." She stole a look at Ethan to see if her remark pleased him, but he appeared not to have heard so she sank back into the seat with a little sigh of resignation.

"They're very lucky, Miss Peterson," John spoke up warmly, "to have such a fine lady as yourself watching over them."

Urliss smiled at the compliment, again glancing at Ethan to see if he concurred with John's appraisal of his good fortune; but he was preoccupied with the radio, twisting the dial and coaxing forth the "devil music" to which Urliss had already assigned American rock.

They arrived early. As the bleachers filled up, Urliss saw several familiar faces. She smiled and waved and called, "Yah, ve're here to vatch our Kip and cheer de Ordlow boys!" With euphoric pleasure she decided that everyone was looking at her and admiring her, so she felt awfully important when the band swooped into El Capitan and imagined herself heading up a parade while the crowd roared approval.

Ethan had brought his field glasses, but it was Urliss who monopolized them, peeping anxiously at the field through the lens, inquiring at two-minute intervals, "Vere's Kipper? Hm? I don't see him."

"He's not playing yet," Ethan explained patiently each time.

When the opposition had gained two touchdowns and had intercepted the ball from Ordlow at the onset of the second quarter, Urliss assessed the groans of despair from the home bleachers and grew convinced that there was some conspiracy brewing against Kip. And possibly against her and Ethan and John also.

"Vy dey not play Kipper?" she demanded through white, even teeth that chattered in the crisp cold.

"Because that clod of a coach has rocks in his head!" Ethan growled sarcastically.

"Dat's vat I tink!" Urliss cried triumphantly. Within the next few minutes her pique mushroomed so that her breathing became quick and heavy, her nostrils flared and white. In her mind she envisioned the coach as a dense, grudge-bearing little despot. "I find dat coach!" she stormed finally.

"Aw, for Pete's sake, Urliss." Ethan glared at her.

She turned on him in a blaze of indignation. "You vant Kip should play ball? I tell dat clod of a coach!" She hadn't the foggiest notion of "clod," but Ethan's tone had matched her mood when he said it.

Ethan looked at her closely, his expression wary and sullen. "Urliss, you'd only embarrass Kip, and Mack would probably never play him all season. Spin down, okay?"

"Ve see!" But she remained uncertainly in her seat, looking in vain for number eighty-one in the field. When the band played at half-time, she shut her ears and stared straight ahead in stony silence. By now her imagination permitted a variety of violent dialogue between herself and the Ordlow coach, between light and darkness, good and evil. And when Dunsmuir scored again in the third quarter, her face grew tight with anger. They were losing the game because the coach was too stubborn to put Kip in! She would do something about that!

While Ethan and John stared and wondered, she plowed through the bleachers, oblivious to wrenched arms and popping heads. She slipped under the rope and scanned the bench for Kip—there he was with all the other forsaken ones—then paused in the heat of her rage to study the important-looking men on the sidelines. Spying a short, husky, balding man yelling at the boys in the field, she demanded of a nearby player, "Is dat de Ordlow coach, hmm?"

"Sure is. That's MacDougal." His grin faded to confusion before her threatening posture.

With a martial gait in her new boots that quickly devoured the distance between them, Urliss confronted MacDougal. His thick, good-looking face was taut but impassive. Distress showed in worried eyes and a tight underlip, but Urliss was blind to the signs of his tension. "You vant to lose de game?" she yelled. "Vy you not play Kipper?"

MacDougal stopped pacing while he stared at her, first in confusion, then with growing incredulity. "Because we're losing already!" he snapped.

Urliss rebounded. "You bumble-head! I command you, put Kip in and see Ordlow vin!"

MacDougal's face gathered into clotted thunderheads. "Ma'am," his voice measured with strained patience. "You'd better leave now."

But Urliss was riding the crest of her temper. "Kip is a good boy and strong!" She groped to further express her outrage and lapsed into a stream of Norwegian.

MacDougal drew himself up to full height so that the top of his head was level with hers and bellowed: "We'll take care of our own ball game, ma'am. We're having enough problems without some batty Swede making more!" He turned and, with giant strides, put the distance back between them.

Her anger fell away and humiliation took its place. A silence had fallen across the bench. Sudden tears made a dark alley for Urliss's vision. She turned with as much dignity as she could muster and picked her stumbling way back to the car. Inside she folded into the cold, red seat, shivering and sobbing.

She hated Ordlow. She hated the prairie. She hated America. Tomorrow she would go back—back to Norway.

But what would her brothers say? Each day they would look at her with sad, pitying eyes and she would die a little within.

Well, then, she would go to San Francisco. There she would find a rich husband. She would show them all.

But her weeping crescendoed to muffled wailing. It was useless. She was just a big Norwegian with a hot temper, and no rich man would want her, not even a poor clerk in some ten-cent store.

Her self-pity knew no bounds. She blew her nose until her hanky was wringing wet; she sat shivering through the last quarter of the ball game, lacking even the vigor to get aroused over the fact that Ethan and John had never come to look for her. If she died no one would miss her.

Ethan did not come until the game was over and then he dawdled around with the car door open so he could covertly examine Urliss under the dome light. She wanted to snap, "Shut de door; can you see I freeze?" But she moved meekly forward in her seat so John could get in back, remaining as mute as the Dunsmuir dummy that Ordlow had burned in effigy.

"Man, it's winter in here," Ethan said heartily as he started the engine.

John agreed. He, too, was more jovial than usual.

"So they know," Urliss thought. "Everyone knows I made a fool's scene." While they crawled into the torturously slow procession leaving the gate, she longed to fade into the dark dashboard.

Ethan said, "Our boys did all right in the last quarter."

"It took them a while to warm up," John said. "I have a hunch they'll play Kip the next time."

"Write and tell me about it, will you, John?" Ethan invited.

"Sure will. I'll drop you a line now and then."

Back at the ranch Urliss went up to her room and locked the door. It was a pretty room, all furnished in tones of blue with a thick oval rug that Mrs. Kettrie had braided out of blue wool shirts and trousers and scarves and neckties.

She pulled off her boots. Too tired to hang up her clothes, she tossed them over a chair with the new suede jacket. She was full of long sighs. With the heat and power of rage gone out of her, she was as empty as a shattered cup. She turned the covers back, got into bed and pulled the lamp chain.

Never had the land spoken its song more poignantly than now. It spoke through the wind flinging dust like pebbles against her window, shuffling around the eaves like children sobbing.

Sleep now, she commanded, sealing her eyes tightly. But mocking little visions gnawed at her thoughts. She opened her eyes and let them bore into the dark as reproaches stabbed her like little needles. One for herself, two for coach MacDougal, three for the uncle who had built the bridge for her dream of coming to America.

3

The Buddies

I'd give my money and half my pride
for a faithful buddy at my side. . . .

WHEN ANNA CAME OUT OF the schoolhouse, the wind pelted dust into her eyes, seamed from staring all summer long into the blinding oracle in the sky. From their harvest in the cornfield, the community brothers had started to sing, their lyrics giving wings to Anna's spirit so that she mouthed the words in a tottering monotone: "If you want joy you must sing for it. . . ."

She had almost forgotten the past now, the running gutters of despair, the mocking devils that had flogged the woof and warp of her mind. Now she was clean washed all the way through, now she had joy.

Heading toward the meadow where Samson, the pet steer, was butting a wobbly fence post, she thought about how they must fix that post; they had been warned to keep the barbed wire strong where it joined the vast Garstin ranch. But Martha was shrieking at her from the schoolhouse above, and the wind snatched her words away so that Anna had to strain her ears and hold her breath in order to hear. " . . . clean hay . . . stables . . . I have everything. . . . " Martha was an afflicted extension of her biblical progenitor. Industrious, thrifty and clean, she was frustrated by the lazy indifference of some of the brothers and sisters and tried to set a right example by working from sun-up till dusk as if chased by demons, taking time out only for prayers that were no doubt full of tensions and complainings.

Anna sighed. In the toolshed that served now as a temporary barn, she picked up the pitchfork and climbed to the loft where she attacked the hay bales half-heartedly. In a moment the swish of fresh hay falling to the manger below made her smile dream-ily. Little swirls of dust spiraled up from the disturbed hay, and the air at the roof was hot and oppressive. A glance through the loft door gave her a glimpse of Samson in the Garstin pasture.

The sight sent her heart to her stomach and she frantically scuttled down the ladder, ripping Samson's halter from its hook. She ran to the side door and yelled at her brothers through cupped hands, waving the halter ominously. "Garstin's land! Samson's on Garstin's land!"

But the brothers were harmonizing: "Ha ha ha, ho ho ho, I will walk without fear before proud men and the devil . . . ha ha ha. . . . " With the wind against her she could not hope to pene-trate their boastful chorus, so she whirled uncertainly through the meadow after the runaway pet. "Come back, you rascal!" She screamed over her shoulder, hoping still that the brothers would hear and run to her aid with their brave songs and long legs.

Samson paid no attention; he kicked his heels and frisked playfully over the open range.

"Somebody'll make hamburger outta you!" Anna called, "or you'll get trampled by a herd of bulls!" She chased him until a sharp knife seemed to chop at her side and the halter was drag-ging at her hand and her breath came in gasps and hitches. Tears stung her eyes as she prayed, "Lord, send Samson back to me, so we won't have any trouble, so we can live here in peace." The prayer was born in a premonition of trouble even before a horse and rider came barreling toward her from the skyline.

A little shaking started in Anna's toes and worked on up into her shoulders. If this were the owner of the ranch, how should she handle it? She had heard that Garstin was a World War II hero, that he wore his pride like Pharaoh's crest, that he was "against little people," a charge evolving from his contempt for the brash souls who trampled the costly pearls of tradition.

If Anna had any preconceived notions about how Garstin might look, she was unprepared for the giant who reined up in front of her now, fair-haired and proud, his mouth full and un-smiling in his square, strong face, his steel-gray eyes boring right into her from under shaggy brows, the force of his presence add-ing a dimension of awe to Anna's timid nature. This, then, was the nobleman without God. She had heard of such men, kings in their own right who exuded a sort of charisma that aroused admiration from the less confident and fear and hatred from their peers; but this was the first time she had ever met one face to face. "I'm awfully sorry," she apologized weakly, her throat dry as a biscuit, "the calf slipped the fence, but we'll get right to fixing it; it won't happen again."

Garstin did not even seem to notice her. With a gesture of controlled annoyance he turned his fleet black stallion after the mischievous hereford. After a swift chase he roped the struggling, bawling Samson with deft movements and pulled him back to where Anna stood with pounding heart.

"Keep him out of here," his voice was soft and gruff.

"Oh, I will—and I'm sorry, honest; thanks for your help, thanks ever so much!" With stumbling fingers she pushed Samson's head into the halter, and recognition made the calf docile. As Garstin dismounted and removed his rope from the steer's neck, Anna watched him closely, observing that everything about him declared a sense of power and authority. As he mounted again and rode away, his horse pranced and snorted like a wild steed. Feeling very small and dejected, Anna led the calf in the direction of the commune, the old sensations of fear and depression tugging at her heart so that it grew tight and heavy. "Help me, Lord Jesus, I'm falling back, help me." But the sorrow persisted.

Back at the make-shift barn she led Samson into his stall and locked the gate. "You can just stay there," she said petulantly, "you're no use to anyone and a lot of trouble." Ever so slowly she made her way back to the schoolhouse, feeling very old and tired, too spent to tell the brothers about Samson breaking fence and Mr. Garstin intercepting him.

In the big room where the smells of supper and the clatter of the redeemed gathering blended roughly, the first thing Anna saw was Betty nursing her baby right out in the open. She turned away with jealous anger.

The baby's coming had made all the brothers soft and thoughtful, and they took turns hovering over him and blessing him. His name was Gideon, and he was full of peace and bliss.

The fanatics had taken in the slim stick of a girl before they

had learned that she was pregnant; but when they had later observed that Betty was carrying a child, they only became increasingly solicitous of her and were glad that she wanted to keep her
child, praying often that a good man would marry her and be a
father to the babe. Meantime they all cuddled him and called
him "nephew."

Furtively Anna watched for those moments when she could
hold the baby, those times when the proud mother would turn
away, smiling secretly to herself—for she had been undone with
love, first the brothers and sisters and then her dear Jesus, and
now this miraculous child—while a passing auntie or uncle admired Gideon, clucking at him or praying for him. Those times
Anna would snatch up the child and hold his warm little body
close to her skinny chest as she danced in swaying circles and
never ceased kissing him.

But jealousy crept unwittingly into her heart and made her
miserable and crochety like a skulking bandit. So intense was
she now that she stormed to her bed and lay down and pulled the
cover over her head, curling tightly into a ball and setting her
face against "This World." She stared inward at her crouching
darkness, that darkness that was devouring her new-found light,
leading her back to that almost forgotten trail from Seattle, from
that neat, two-story house on Azee street that she had called
home for seventeen years.

It had always been a house full of long, whispery sighs. Her
mother and father had sighed the evenings away in front of the
Waltons or on the back stoop, their faces lax and dull as if they
had been born old and sorrowful and the passing years had only
confirmed what they had known at birth—that life was a cup of
bitter herbs spoon-fed to their wasting souls. It was not the great
tragedies that ruined them for meaningful living but the mun-
dane trickle of little griefs and disappointments, so that if Anna
asked advice for anything, their response was forever gloomy.
"Expect nothing," their spirits said, "for here we are, look at us,
ah, the dreams we had. . . . " And they would retire into their
shell of breathing death, shaking their heads sadly.

Often their grief expressed itself through sorrowful eyes that
followed their plain, bitter daughter with resignation to this,
their final misfortune; Anna would feel their disappointment and

her own bruised psyche would crash so that she had to get away.

But where could she go? Her few friends would turn away if she talked to them about how she hurt inside, like pebbles being dropped into a frail, thin pouch that was getting twisted and misshapen and ready to burst. But then she went off to college and on the rampage, shedding her bruised spirit and her bi-focals at the same time. That was when she had met Barry who had swept her off her feet and used her like an old towel, quickly tiring of her, leaving her more hurt and twisted than ever. And that was the beginning of her wanderings through one town after another, trying to find herself and her place and getting quieter and more withdrawn with passing time.

She was hitching a ride in downtown Los Angeles when Brother Ben had found her (one of those haunted ones, he would say later) and had introduced her to Jesus. It was as if the real Anna had been curled up in an old barrel of sludge and someone had come along and lifted her up and cleaned her off and set her on a new path. Through her awakened spirit she experienced God the Creator becoming her Savior; and, ever since, He had been her tender companion, molding her into His own child. It was a daily experience which filled her with such awe sometimes that she would stop whatever she was doing to wonder how He who made the worlds could commune with a plain, dull-witted girl like herself.

But since Betty's baby had come, she was surprised time and again at the sponge-like capacity of her being for hungers and longings that never would be filled—surprised, too, that the darkness came back sometimes.

"Anna, Anna, what's wrong?" It was Elder Brother Ben speaking as he bent over her. Feeling his firm, kindly hand on her shoulder, she yearned to hurl herself into his arms and lean into his manly strength and find comfort.

Instead she hid her puffy, swollen face deeper into the pillow and tried to stifle her sobs by holding her breath.

"Anna, shall I call one of the sisters?"

She lifted her head and said fiercely, "Isn't there any privacy in this place?" She hiccoughed, her tongue swabbing the hot salt tears leaking through her lips.

Brother Ben stood as if to leave. "I'm sorry for breaking in."

Anna lifted her head and stared sideways at the wall.

"After I found Jesus I quit hating myself, but now I'm at it again. . . . " She broke into fresh sobs, flouncing her head once more onto the pillow so that she could not tell him the rest—how she longed for a husband and child and was not worthy of a good man even if one should want her.

Again elder brother placed his hand on her shoulder, and Anna would be grateful later that he did not talk about how God looks only on the heart, how to Him she was very beautiful. Instead he started to sing, very softly, so that his voice vacillated between a whisper and a tone.

"Who will build your kingdom, Lord?
The poor, the wretched, the sad,
Who will be your children, Lord?
The misfits, outcasts, the bad. . . ."

And suddenly she could recognize the Comforter. He was all around her, filling her up with love; gentle, tender power, washing over her so that soon through her tears her heart was singing. Groping for a hanky under her pillow she blew her nose. "I'm so ashamed, I don't know what gets into me sometimes."

"In the Christ-life we grow day by day, year after year," elder brother said; "we learn through our stumblings." His face was kind and shining. "How about going with me tomorrow to sell our potatoes?"

"I'd like that," she said, smiling in spite of her crimson nose.

Only last week they had discovered that the potato crop was all that stood between them and hunger, so ten of their men had gone off to work with a government dam building project sixty miles west. And now they had decided to market only thirty sacks of potatoes at a roadside stand and save the rest for their winter food.

But the next day Brother Ben had to repair the water pump, and he asked Bobby to go with Anna in his stead.

"I don't have my head together," Bobby declined. "I don't wanta go."

"Do you always do what you want?" elder brother asked.

Bobby thought about that; with great reluctance he yielded. Although he was recovering from some of his hang-ups,

Bobby still had social problems. Here in this family unit he felt snug and secure, but it seemed to him that the design of those on the outside was to hurt him. On those rare occasions when he ventured to town, he kept his face down, and when he raised his eyes they were filled with little fears and pleadings. Don't hurt me, he seemed to be begging; stand back and don't hurt me.

He knew that some day he and all the others would have to leave this family and go out into the world to bind up the brokenhearted and preach liberty to the prisoners; but whenever someone alluded to this bend in the road, Bobby grew timid and quiet.

Small and frail, with a full red beard which he supposed made him appear more masculine, he played the harmonica with such melancholy flair that Anna thought she had heard the songs somewhere long ago. Often she watched the way Bobby's long, knotted fingers with the light red hairs around the knuckles cupped the organ. His eyes looked far off as if he was seeing his daddy who was in jail or his little sister who had died from leukemia or the convalescent hospital where he first came off drugs. She had heard about how Bobby was playing the harmonica in his grandmother's yard one day and he had started walking out the gate and over the hill and never looked back, never turned around, just kept walking and hitching rides and playing the harmonica clear across six states.

Anna and Bobby and Martha and Betty and Annabelle were the only singles in the commune, but somehow it was Bobby that Anna felt the sorriest for. He was such a helpless baby.

After the brothers had loaded the old pickup with the potatoes, Bobby and Anna rode out and parked it on a turn-off about a quarter-mile from the truck stop. The day was mellow with a languor that drifted over the funeral pyre of stubble in the distant fields and the golden grassland.

They set up their sign: New Potatoes by Gunny Sack, $4.00. Right away a nice lady with several small children stopped and bought a sack, which Bobby loaded into her station wagon, thanking her four or five times.

And then they waited. Occasionally a car went by but no one stopped. After a while Anna decided to walk down to the truck stop on the pretext of getting a drink, although she was mostly restless and urged by the desire to move around. While she was gone Bobby sat idly on the pickup bumper, anxious and apprehensive from habit, trying to steer his thoughts into positive channels as he went over the scripture he had memorized and then endeavoring to pray. "Praise God," he whispered, "praise the Lord. I see Him high and lifted up. . . . "

There was much work to be done. King Jesus would soon be coming. Man, what a sight that would be when He came crashing through the split sky with a million angels cheering. Already Brother Conrad was going out to the cities of the nation preaching love and repentance because the kingdoms of this world would soon belong to Christ forever. "Prepare for the Bridegroom!" Conrad was thundering like Jeremiah of old! "Judgment begins at the house of God! Love your neighbors, give all that you don't need to the poor!"

A car pulled up and four young men in cowboy boots and Levi jackets got out. Tall and lanky with impish faces, they smelled to Bobby of old, remembered dangers. "Mind if we look at your spuds?" one of them asked, feeding his mouth a pinch of snuff. The hairs following his jaw were long and downy as if coddled with a soft brush.

"N-no, sir," Bobby said quickly, "you go right ahead." The little nerve above his brow started twitching erratically. His timid eyes did not pursue the young men as they examined his potatoes, murmuring exaggerated praise over the size and color. Instead, he sat with rigid calm and stared at the fine line where earth and sky fell together. Only when a cascade of potatoes hit the ground did it occur to him that his fears were realized: the young men were cutting the strings on the gunny sacks and turning them upside down. Bobby froze, his brain, like his muscles, congealing so that he could only continue to stare at the horizon.

One by one they emptied the sacks, sending the potatoes scurrying like bouncing balls. Still Bobby could only look on in frozen terror, the strength in him falling away like a tide going out to sea. He heard shrill little cries like a mewing kitten and saw Anna wade into the heap like a streak of lightning as she sought to salvage the scurrying cargo. "Don't!" she shrieked. "Please don't!"

But their work was done now and they considered her with

narrow amusement as she knelt at their feet and plucked potatoes back into an empty sack.

Bobby was a petrified block on the bumper. Surely God would punish them, he thought hopefully; surely He would strike them down.

But God was silent.

So he must protect his sister, he must act at once. "How come this little lady's hiding out from our world," one of the renegades was saying; "nice-lookin' broad like this oughta make it anywhere."

"Them religious kooks must keep her happy; wonder how they do it."

Anna hung her head even lower so that her hair parted at her shoulders, exposing her thin, vulnerable neck. With jerky motions Bobby moved to help her, squatting beside her as he went to work.

"Well, lookit that; who said these religious fanatics ain't gentulmen? Clint, you turkey, did you say that? Well, you're dead wrong, lookit this dude helping his girl here."

"Cowards and draft-card burners, maybe." another voice chimed in, "but like you say, real gentulmen."

"I'd have to see under the beard t'know for sure."

"Well, Len here's the best beard trimmer in the country; got your horse clippers, Len? Hey, gentulman, we wanta see your face. You don't mind, do ya?"

Bobby acted as if he had not heard. With numb, mechanical fingers he continued his chore, counting the potatoes under his breath. " . . . sixteen, eighteen, twenty-two . . . ."

When they grabbed him and flipped him over, he turned his eyes inward and went on counting . . . twenty-eight . . . , his hands fluttering idly, his legs convulsed under the weight of their buttocks, making no resistance at all, opening his eyes just once to glimpse the long shears snipping roughly at his fine red beard and Anna's streaming eyes thrust briefly over the circle before she was roughly shoved away. "Don't, oh, don't," she kept pleading, like an actress doing her lines over and over.

" . . . forty-five, forty-six, forty-seven. . . . "

Finally someone did stop, someone whose voice fell like a whiplash across the mischievous deed. And Bobby's tormentors fled like jackals slinking from the prey.

Slowly Bobby staggered to his feet, feeling with trembling hand the stubble on his chin as he peered at his benefactor, a big man whose gaze passed inscrutably over him and Anna and the strewn potatoes.

"Better clean up this mess and get home," he said, his voice gruff. He crossed the highway and got back into his black Lincoln and drove away.

It took a long time to toss all the potatoes into the truck box, even the broken and bruised ones, but when the task was done they struck out for the commune.

"If I'd had more faith in the Lord, if I hadn't been so fearful, it maybe wouldn't have happened," Bobby finally suggested, choking with self-contempt.

"It's always gentle people who are picked on by bullies," Anna said through chattering lips, unable to stop shivering even though the cab was warm. "They would never pick on someone who could defend himself, someone as mean as they are!" She clasped her trembling hands together. "Did you see how they scattered when Mr. Garstin came!"

Bobby, who was still trying to collect his wits, mused, "So that was him."

"There's something about that man I admire," Anna said. "That's twice he's helped me."

"M-maybe we should do him a favor; but what would it be?"

But Anna had grown introspective, shutting Bobby out from some brooding spot in her mind. "You know we have to pray for those bullies, don't you?" She asked. "You know that Jesus said to love those who wrong you and forgive them from your heart."

"Tell me that when I lay dyin'," Bobby said. A minute later he added, "At least let me get my wind." He sucked in his breath and whooshed it out again. "Man, I hate people like that; they make life miserable for everybody." He sighed again. "But if Jesus wants me to love 'em, well, I'll give Him my will; He'll have to do the rest."

"Brother Ben says we'll never build peace in the world till we do the job in our own backyards," Anna said with feeling, shivering now with righteousness. "Bobby, are you all right? How do you feel?"

He grinned weakly. "Not too bad, Annie girl; feel like I'm getting my head together, like maybe I can sell potatoes again someday."

"Bobby, that's the best thing I've ever heard you say. You hear that, Lord? You've got a good hold on Bobby." She continued to shake with feeling.

They drove into the yard and Bobby turned off the ignition. The sounds of clattering dishes and a strumming guitar floated out from the open schoolhouse window, over the garden and cornfield and grass—all bowing and limping back to the sod, over the charred remains of the barn at the edge of the yard, black, ugly thing that it was, a reminder of trial and loss. It was dinner time.

Anna and Bobby looked at each other and smiled because their family would be waiting for them with lentil soup, piping hot, and fresh whole-grain bread and custard, and after they had finished eating someone would ask whatever happened to Bobby's beard, and Anna would tell them about the nasty episode and then they would all file into the big room for prayer and worship. And after they had prayed, God was apt to do something special, like bringing those cowards here with a sore conscience and a hunger to know about His love for them. Anna giggled. "Those bullies don't know what they're up against with us prayin' for them."

Bobby tried to grin. "They haven't seen the power of the Lord in action," he agreed, "M-maybe it'll blow 'em into the kingdom!"

4

His Brother's Keeper

He said, Feed my sheep,
the lambs are a'cryin;
the ewes are a'dyin'—
He said, If you love me. . . .

THIS WEEK would gain a footnote in the archives of Shellydown for suitcase-jamming, what with Urliss packing hers at
least three times, muttering about "football coach" and "vilderness" while she emptied everything from her closet into the trunk
she had brought from Norway. Each time she examined Kip's
reaction and wept softly for the "poor boy's pale, terrified face"
—although Kip looked as pleasant and composed as ever—and
unloaded everything back into the closet, winding up the whole
exercise by leaving part of her wardrobe in the trunk just in case
there be "vun bit more of insolence" to drive her forth forever
from this monstrous hinterland.

Ethan stuffed his own luggage, Kip's pullman and his father's
old duffel bag as his list of college needs grew. As Ethan's date of
departure neared, Urliss insisted that John move into the house
instead of waiting for the snow to fly as he usually did; so the
hired hand politely trudged upstairs to the spare room, his grips
bulging with boots and Levis and socks which he sorted and
heaved into the old solid walnut dresser with its sticky drawers
and stained mirror and its one short leg balanced with a copy of a
Sears sale catalog.

Waking to the sound of yodeling in the shower one morning,
Kip remembered that after today those vocal tremors would be
far away along with all his brother's habits that were as familiar

to him as his own hands. He felt as if his stomach had turned into a gnarled rope, all heavy and twisted, and his covers had been stripped away under a canopy of cold eyes staring at his lonely nakedness. Rolling feet first out of bed, he stumbled into ragged jeans and bounded down the outside stairs in one breath. At the garage he washed Ethan's car and dried it with a chamois. Then he carted his suitcases down and arranged them neatly in the trunk.

When Ethan came out, stepping to the rhythm of Urliss's list of warnings—"Remember to set alarm, don't vash T-shirts vid coloreds, breakfast is most important meal"—he was munching on a cinnamon roll while he pondered the familiar sights sprawling before him: the windmill screeching like an old bat, the barn protruding against the horizon like a fat sentinel, and his docile mare, Polly, head hung low over the grass now turned white. Kip stared hard at him. He remembered the little mole behind his ear that showed up after a fresh haircut and the veins which stood up like little blue ridges on his arms.

Ethan grinned, wiping his hands roughly on his handkerchief. "Well, it's high time we're splitting our act."

"Yeah, it's weaning time," Kip agreed cheerfully. "You're gettin' too dependent on me. Minnesota'll make a man out of you."

Ethan patted the car door. "Thanks for cleaning this baby. I'll raise your pay next time." He cuffed at Kip's shoulder and slid onto the seat. "Well, so long."

Kip gave a mock salute. He watched the Ford stir dust down the lane and turn onto the county road, watched until it was hidden by the hill. "So long," he whispered, his shoulders heavy. He went back upstairs.

Ethan's room smelled like old leather and shaving lotion. Some of his personal effects were stripped—the banners that their folks had brought home from their travels had left darker areas on the painted walls; the little chest that their father had carved one rainy afternoon, and the brass statue that Ethan had won at the State Fair for first place in the three-mile race event were gone from their usual places. Otherwise everything looked just the same—the rumpled bedspread with its threadbare Indian head, the table radio with a dusty tube balanced on top of its case and the oval picture of the brothers in their cowboy hats and boots taken at a Fourth-of-July rodeo when they were in grade school. Kip stood in the doorway for a minute and then he went back out, the coiled rope in his stomach getting bigger and tighter so that when he reached the outside landing, it seemed that all the squalling, bawling life of the ranch revealed itself to him with nostalgia wrapped in anguish.

But John took the edge off Kip's loneliness. Not only was he a weaver of stories, but his menagerie of friends came with mysterious airs to stand awkwardly inside the front door, to shuffle their feet and look timidly around as they waited for him to finish shaving or choring or whatever it was that was keeping him.

John would visit casually with his guests in the house until the stove had taken the chill out of his bunkhouse, and then he would lead them out there where they could visit in private. Once he put in an extra cot for Louis Mertes, the lost Mexican, who came sometimes to stay the night. Others came, too, their tinny cars grinding slowly through the lane with dimmed headlights and clapping mufflers. John attracted outcasts like some kind of pied piper.

Lucy Harness was one of them. She had come, her pretty face tucked into a red knit scarf.

"You have babies vid you?" Urliss inquired politely but coolly from the kitchen where she was cleaning the stove.

"The car is warm," Lucy replied shyly, as if that explained everything, twisting her gloves nervously.

"Dey might get gassed," Urliss warned.

Lucy looked alarmed.

Kip laughed. "There's no problem for a few minutes," he said, "but bring them in if you want."

About then they heard John's boots stomping on the back step and Lucy turned anxiously to meet him.

It was common knowledge that Lucy was a good wife and mother most of the time, that she loved her children with quiet desperation. Except some Saturday nights, when she went to parties and got carried away at the refreshment corner, turning into some sort of witch and causing enough scandal to satisfy the whole community's sense of outraged decency until the next Saturday night.

"She psycho," Urliss decided.

"She needs help," John agreed.

Urliss gave him a hard look. "She need a good spank!" She slammed the cupboard door shut.

John sighed. "Mostly she needs our prayers."

"You pray for her!" Urliss yelled at him. "I pray for her husband!" She started kneading her bread, but her anger mounted with every "plop-plop-plop."

"Vat are you, a jelly brain?" she demanded of John. "Do you not see you must stand absolute, not show indifference to sin. How else shall children know how to live!"

But one day Lucy's face took on a bright, clean shine and she looked prettier than ever. Even Urliss noticed the change. Their friends claimed that Lucy and her husband were plumb silly about each other since John had converted them both to Christ and they had joined his church, spending so much time there that there just wasn't room for Saturday night parties. Kip appraised John with mounting respect, and Urliss grudgingly acknowledged his "vay vid peoples."

But John was on the firing line. Even as he helped the fanatics to build a shelter that would replace the burned barn, a meeting was being organized by troubled Ordlowites to harangue about the commune.

"They're going to run the fanatics out and John along with them!" Kip called to Urliss one day as he hurried by the porch where she was sweeping the floor.

"Vat you say!" she demanded, although Kip was sure she had understood what he had told her.

"John," he repeated, "he's not very popular just now." He turned around to face her, walking backward. "Some folks want to railroad him. Why would anyone want to hurt a good man like John?"

"How shall I know?" she cried angrily, glowering at him. "Does it not happen to good men each day—but in America!" Her face became pale and frightened. "Life be a riddle, I say—de longer I live, de less I know!"

"Yep. Well, if my dad were here there'd be no danger." He turned to open the gate.

"He is a fool, dat John!" Urliss called after him. Agitation quickened her movements until she was almost running. Reaching one end of the porch, she swept the floor in a frenzy of wasted motion, and when she had finished, swept it again.

Kip jumped into the jeep and gunned the motor. He was off to give John and the fanatics a hand putting a roof on the new shelter.

Although the material and workmanship were crude, the sisters kept coming out to admire the new structure, as long as a boxcar; nodding and smiling their approval, they dragged mattresses and bedrolls onto the bare floor, setting up a sort of housekeeping before the partitions were even finished.

Kip recognized one of them as the girl he had seen on the night of the barn fire. Today there was only a trace of the haunted look about her, and when she smiled, as she did now, her face lit up so that Kip found himself staring at her with puzzled admiration. "Hi, there," he called to her, smiling. She smiled back, her face flushing with sudden shyness that Kip found delightful. Reluctantly he watched her walk away until the schoolhouse had swallowed her up again.

While Kip pounded nails into the slanted roof, the brothers showed their gratitude by bringing him cold water at regular intervals. He was able to study them firsthand, deciding that their soft eyes gazing out of bearded faces made them appear childlike and transparent, as if they had always known a world of tented fields and cornstalks glistening in the sun, far removed from the purgatory of rebels and misfits. From time to time they played pranks on one another, doubling over with uninhibited laughter.

Once while they were taking time out, Brother Ben sat beside Kip and John and told them a little about his dreams. "Someday I'd like to have a ranch here for kids who don't have a decent place to lie down," he said, the look of a trailblazer crossing his wide-set eyes and square jaw. "I hope in time to win the confidence of good people in this area, who'd back us for more land."

Kip smiled sympathetically. "The poor fool," he thought kindly, "he's got no sense about dry-land farming, doesn't even know that forty acres on the prairie isn't enough to grow a good garden without irrigation. So they'll starve, and he'll find out then that his notion about a youth ranch is pretty dumb." But he asked with interest, "How did you happen to land here?" and listened carefully as Ben told his story.

"Rich Parker and I worked in the St. Louis ghettos and then in an underground station for runaway youngsters, trying to rehabilitate them. We'd take as many as seven at a time into our house and talk to them about Christ. Without Him we could never've pulled them up from their problems. Even then the results were slow, but gloriously real, and the numbers grew out-of-bounds.

"I knew the youngsters needed a live-in situation where they could be loved and lifted and taught in a family environment. And we all wanted to put as much distance between us and the dirty air and crowding as we could. We didn't plan to come this far north," he added, almost apologetically, "but at one time we played with the idea of an Alaskan base.

"It was through someone John had helped that we learned he'd welcome us here, and that bit of news came as a sort of confirmation to my dream of a prairie being the place where the deep scars in these kids could heal. There's something about these open spaces, the big sky, and each person as important as a king that helps make it happen."

Kip blinked his confusion. He wondered how any of them could be helped if they were resisted and disliked by the local people. That kind of rejection was liable to offset any good that Ben and Rich and the big old prairie could hope to muster.

"When they're ready," Ben was saying, "We'll send them back into society as good neighbors and citizens. We'll send them out and other needy souls will come in to replace them."

Kip smiled and nodded sympathetically, pushing what he had just learned through his mind as he hammered nails with a fresh burst of energy.

As the afternoon wore on, a battered sedan groaned into the driveway. Its occupants slowly crawled out to stand self-consciously, their hands jammed into thin jacket pockets, looking toward the shelter where the brothers were working. Kip could tell that the newcomers were dirty in their tight, scroungy jeans and matted hair. From every direction the brothers and sisters descended on them, holding them in their long, skinny arms as they spoke soft words of welcome. Their warmth made the visitors respond with eagerness, except for one who broke down and tried to articulate his desperation through dry, wrenching sobs. "There now, Jesus loves you, we love you." Gently they led their new friends into the schoolhouse.

If the scene puzzled Kip and annoyed him, it also made a deep impression on him. That evening he told John that he thought the whole furor over the commune was a witch hunt.

John said nothing but he looked pleased as he stretched and groaned comfortably. He had come to love Kip; he felt that Kip was a young prince. And then he thought about his own son and how he might have been a lot like Kip if John hadn't failed somewhere.

Always when he reached this far into the past, his brows struggled to battle and his face collapsed into seams of pain. He tried to figure out just where he had gone wrong with young Johnny.

Once he had tried to tell Mr. Kettrie a little about him; it had been Ethan's ninth birthday and Kettrie had bought him a small bike. "When my boy was a youngster he was wild about ships," John had told him, "so I made him a little boat with seven sails. Well, sir, he liked that boat, hitched it to a length of twine and sailed it on the irrigation ditch at the Reservation all summer long; nights he kept it by his bed—a cute little tyke, husky like Ethan there. . . ."

But it was useless, he could not talk about his son, although Kettrie had encouraged him with, "That so! Got any snaps of him, John?"

"Packed away," John had said, his voice trailing off. To take out the snapshots of Johnny from the bottom flap of his old trunk would bring him a taut throat all wattled with his face turned close to the wall and grief burning away the sleepless hours while Johnny called to him from that carefully sealed off room in the gray abyss of all his remembering.

"Pa, hey, Pa!"

"Good to see you so happy, Johnny! Why are you singing and shouting, why are you dancing with the broom? Put the broom away and we'll go fishing."

"Sadie's gonna marry me, Pa!"

"That's fine, fine. She's a nice girl."

"My wild days are over. I'm gonna settle down, be a family man, make you proud."

"Son, I'm proud of you, always was."

"Naw, you're lyin'. I gave you a lot of grief. But I'll straighten out, honest, Pa, I swear it! . . ."

"Honest, Judge, I swear it, I just hit 'im a hard right to the jaw, wasn't my fault his head hit the bar; feel plumb rotten about it, but he went out with my girl. We were gonna be married, so I hit 'im. . . . "

Hush falls like a dark cape over the courtroom. You twist your neck and blink hard in order to see your son as they bring him in, that scarecrow of ragged limbs and face working confusion like pistons as it shrinks before the crowd, feeling currents of hate like sharp little arrowheads. Like the last swell on the oceantide the crowd murmurs, "He always was a troublemaker. . . . "

". . . If they put me in a cage I'll go ape. . . ."

"There now, Johnny, hold on; we'll make it."

But they're leading Johnny away and he's all squashed into the limp rag of his body, the scrapper gone to sleep beneath the din. The crowd is less hostile how; justice has been done. . . .

Back in the little house by the irrigation ditch where Johnny sailed his boat, where the rooms are dark and stuffy from being sealed away from the sun, you rage through the long, black tunnel inside yourself.

By and by old Zeller comes, his rheumy eyes focused on some half-forgotten memory as he idles the creaking chair where you once sobered him up and sent him to his watchman's shift.

"How old is your boy now, Johnson?"

Like a tired sigh your voice comes up from the cellar. "Twenty-one yesterday."

"Too bad, just a sprig."

"Too bad"—the warden shakes his head from the crumbling tower that echoes the cries of the doomed for centuries—"too bad, he tore some strips from the blanket, hanged himself from the light cord. . . . "

The seasons came and left, spring broke with bits of green

struggling through bogs of mud that sucked at hooves and boots, but John never went back to the Reservation where Johnny lay beside the mama who had given her breath to convulsions while birthing him.

"Come no more," John Rainwater Johnson begged at the sealed-off room where Johnny called to him. His plea caught somewhere in the rafters of his huddled soul and settled on the army of lost children calling brother to the night wind.

On the evening of October tenth, John excused himself from the dinner table after the last bite of krumkake and went upstairs, reappearing later in the hall, smooth-shaven, his boots glinting from fresh polish and wearing his dress coat. To Kip there was something sad about John's grooming himself up so carefully, and when he had left for town Kip said to Urliss, "I think John needs some support tonight—want to go with me?"

"No, I vill not go," she replied, clearing the table with sweeping motions, "and if you had sense you vould not go, eider. It vill shame John more if ve are dere."

"Suit yourself." Kip shrugged into his overcoat and went out to warm up the jeep.

An hour later he bounded into the city hall foyer, hearing a soapbox plea followed by the sound of hands clapping from the room to the right, which he quietly entered, examining the crowd thoughtfully while continuing to listen to the speaker. He took a seat in the back row, sensing a mood that seemed tense and mean and curious all at once. He guessed there were about two hundred grim faces all concentrated on Pat Haber who chaired the meeting in a no-nonsense manner, his glasses flashing in the overhead light above the rostrum. "Asa has been trying to get in a few words," he was saying; "let him at it."

Normally quiet and unassuming, Asa Klinger, who worked a farm so small he was forced to grab odd jobs to support his five children, was now wrought up, moving his weight from one foot to another so that he appeared to be marching to lively music, his hands working with the tempo of his feet, in and out of his jacket pockets, chopping at the air like an ax over a woodpile. "We're going through bad times in this country," he said in a hoarse, guttural voice. "Every five minutes somebody's getting murdered, violated. This great nation's becoming a jungle, and now it's spreading to the little out-of-the-way towns, and you all know why. Because folks like you, Johnson, do-gooders of all shades, are trying to make themselves look like Good Samaritans by aiding criminals and drug addicts." He chopped his hand at John. "It's a known fact you keep strange bedfellows, Johnson. I could say some of your friends belong to the animal kingdom, but that would be an insult to my dog, Rex, and my cow, Tilly, not to mention my pig, Albert—"

"All right, all right, that's enough," Pat Haber said wearily.

"Asa's tellin' it like it is!" someone shouted.

John stood up then, pivoting to face the crowd, and looking (Kip would report later) kindly and unafraid, like an old king defending his broken garrison. He quietly told them, "Those children want fresh air and freedom and a simple life. They want to worship God the way their hearts tell them to. They're not too unlike the first colonists—."

George Pruett jumped to his feet with such force that for a minute he could not spew his words clearly. "You oughta be a—a politician, Johnson, with your 'colonist' fairy tales; those fanatics came outta places decent folks can't imagine—"

"Yes, they've come out of some bad trips," John agreed sadly, "but God has received them; He went seeking after them through good men who are leading them in the way of Christ."

"If they're so good, why're they hiding out from the world? Why aren't they out facing the hard, cold facts like the rest of us!

"You're gullible, John, and dumb, you don't have the power in your brain to light a match—"

Pat Haber pounded the table. "Let's hear from John Whittier," he said as a swell of fresh palavering broke over the crowd.

Whittier was as smooth-looking as he was silk-tongued. When he cleared his throat and turned his head slowly, you could see that he wanted everyone to get a good look at him. Whittier spoke as if choosing his words carefully. "What could a man be thinking of," he murmured, "retreating to a place like this, far from traffic and people and authorities. My friends, we'd have to wonder about his intentions. Is there some treachery afoot? Remember the Reverend Jim Jones? Guyana?"

The entire crowd gasped and broke into a swell of sound.

Whittier held up his hand. "But let's look at the facts. We know for certain that more of these 'hippie' sort of down-and-outers are coming in all the time, and they're on drugs, no matter what they say about kicking the habit. No, we're not out of line in running them clear out of the country. Decent people everywhere are reacting against these—these 'communes.' "

Bernie Fletcher got up, holding his hat politely over his chest, his bowed legs stuffed into western boots and tight Levis. "I always get them hippies confused with Chris's sheep dogs. . . . " The rest of his words were lost in a wave of laughter. "But the way I see it, I don't like John, either. He's a busybody and a nuisance. But we're reputationed hereabouts for being a bunch of whiskey-drinkin', mother-lovin' cowboys and to tar 'n' feather John might damage our reputation. I suggest we deal directly with them hippies, give 'em the word they're not wanted, tell 'em to move on."

"Sic 'em, Bernie!" a friend encouraged him. "Next time we see one o' them long-haired sissies in this here town, he's in for a haircut and a little buckshot in his rompers."

And then Myrna Hatchet came forward, shrinking timidly into her skinny bosom, clutching her purse with long, bloodless fingers, her nearsighted eyes darting nervously.

"All I know—" Myrna cleared her throat and raised her head like a little dog baying at the moon—"all I know is what happened to my boy—you all heard of Dilly—he was born to raise hell just like his dad, in and outta reform school. Well, them folks at the commune showed him a better way to live—no matter what you say—they showed him the Lord, and now he's like an angel from heaven, not the same boy at all; says his prayers at the table and empties the garbage without bein' told. Ain't none of you gonna kick 'im around no more because the Lord takes care o' His own!" She went back to her seat, ducking her head from side to side and picking self-consciously at her coat buttons.

Kip wanted to laugh. This whole business was a circus with the melodramatics snatched from a third-grade drama portraying John Brown and the Feds. But in spite of his amusement, his heart went out to these friends and neighbors who had survived the rebel seasons of this big land, having outfoxed the dry, selfish summers with spirits as tough as the land itself. Drawing strength from deep, elusive springs of moisture through the most fragile of tendrils, their fear of the world outside with its monotonous jungle of schedules and programmed thinking and sheeplike mentality was greater than their fear of privation on the prairie. In their minds it was better to starve in the long snows than surrender to that swinging scythe of conformity that reduced all men to the lowest stature; better to go down under hard-pan than scrounge for the prize of adventure with a briefcase and a pound of fittings in that world out there. They would fight the commune in the same vigorous manner that they resisted the avant-garde mentality and nuclear power pollution. One thing seemed apparent, though, they weren't going to make a martyr out of John, at least at the moment.

5

Fanatics, Get Out

You hurt, Lord?
Because we love our pots and taffy
better than little Tim Brown?

THE DELEGATION carrying the gloomy tidings of dismissal to the commune comprised ten volunteers who formed a train of crawling cars which lent a funeral gravity to the occasion.

Asa Klinger did most of the talking and afterward everyone would agree that he was kindly, sympathetic even, as he explained to the solemn young rebels why their continued presence was apt to ignite the passions of the good people of Ordlow County who worried that the brothers and sisters represented a moral compromise to their sense of integrity. "Now, boys," he said reasonably, "I'm sure you can understand the position of these good men who bear the concerns of this county always on their hearts. The folks in Ordlow are committed to keeping a clean, moral climate for our children to grow in. You folks with your draft-dodgin' ways and your messed-up friends comin' in here are bound to confuse our children. Now we don't want to get tough; none of us likes to get hard-nosed. We don't like telling you to move on, but this is our duty, you understand."

"If we thought we were a threat to the good people around here, we'd be gone tomorrow if we could," Ben said. "We sure want to live as a good example of God's love."

"The youngsters everywhere are practically bringing this nation to its knees, what with their killin' and rapin' and goin' on the public dole. We can't help a lot of that, but we can keep the jungle from coming here," Asa continued.

"It's still a free country," Ben said softly. "There's a lot of room here for the poor leftovers from the cities to find a new life—that's what America is really all about. And we have to care enough to help one another—that's what the Gospel's all about."

"Most of us in these parts look at draft-dodgers like they were slinking coyotes, preying on the labor of honest men who bear arms in the front line when this country needs 'em."

"There's a power greater than bullets, the power of the Spirit of God who moves through our prayers and obedience to Him, enough power to tear down the armies of the enemy."

"—lotta hogwash." Asa swore and spat on the ground. "You're hidin' behind the skirts of your religious excuses." His voice started going upstairs with intensity as he aired his pet peeve. "This country didn't get its freedom without bloodshed, and it won't stay free without it, either. The communist powers are gettin' ready to move on this last stronghold of freedom. If we go down" —he sliced the air with his hand— "the whole world'll follow. Slaves is what we'll be! Oh, you religious nuts'll fare all right. You'll belly up to the commies and sell us down the river—"

"My friend," Ben interrupted gently, "we have a God who can stop their armies in their tracks and make them know that He is our great God and they are our brothers."

The word "brothers" seemed to set Asa into a complete loss of control so that he threw a fit right in front of everybody, cursing and shaking a threatening fist in the general direction of his antagonists who, among other things, "are a lot of crazies!" he yelled. "We're cleaning the trash from our backyard, I'll tell ya that!" And he slouched into his car and whipped away at high speed, leaving the remaining delegates in open-mouthed disarray. One by one they regained their hard, determined composure, revived their own motors and screeched away. "Now see what you've done!" Mattie Carson hollered as she left the bewildered, bearded foe. "He might have a stroke!" She drove off in a flurry of triumph.

Asa did not return immediately to Ordlow where he could trumpet the word of resistance in the enemy camp. First he went to the Garstin ranch where he could bend the ear of that wise and sympathetic maverick.

Dow Garstin was helping his hired men herd cattle to winter pasture when Asa's car came charging and bouncing over a dubious prairie trail, scattering bawling cows and sending their calves into a startled race across the terrain. His impassive features broke into a scowl as he watched the intruder who finally parked the car and ran to him, clutching Dow's stirrup like a doomed prisoner making a desperate bid for clemency. "Got to talk to you, Mr. Garstin!" he cried, releasing a torrent of sound and syllable not nearly so eloquent as the anguish of his knotted face.

"We care, Mr. Garstin," Asa pleaded; "we care about what's happening to our country. People who care have to act; can't sit on our hands while the country goes straight to hell. It's happening right under our noses. *They* say they like it here and don't want to move on. *They* say they're gonna change the system, even turn the church upside down!"

"What the devil are you talking about, Asa?" Dow exploded impatiently.

Asa's face went blank as it became clear to him that his breast-beating appeal had failed to penetrate Dow's understanding. "Why, the commune, man, the commune. Listen, their leader told me in pictures as plain as daylight that they have a commission to make everybody live in peace. He said their mission is to live in tents and call judgment on the materialistic, warring society—you know who he's talkin' about—and make all the churches of America give their money to feed the hordes of India and China and them other cow-worshippers over the face of the globe. You see, they hate the wealth of this great country, hate the military that let's us sleep safe in our beds. They'd sic them slit-eyed buzzards of China on us and help 'em make slaves of us all!"

Dow's expression moved from muted disgust to grim resolve. In spite of Asa's ragged monologue, he understood exactly what he was trying to tell him. He tapped the brim of his hat and slapped his nervous horse to a fast gallop after the receding herd. "I'll look into it," he said over his shoulder.

Moving the cows was slow work and Dow fell to brooding about the commune, which had become a symbol of all the undermining powers at work to destroy the blood-sealed foundation of democracy, a symbol of barbarians who were everywhere, hiding their clanking chains behind brutish habits and dishonest conduct that held out the promise of an easy life. So those young rebels thought they could settle in like reformed bandits, did they? In too many places responsible people had abdicated authority to a mass of hot-eyed young pups who ought to be horse-whipped and sent to work on empty stomachs. Peace sayers, eh? *The cowards.* The more he thought about it, the more his outrage grew; by the time the last hereford had been shut into the slopes of the eastern pasture, Dow had made up his mind to take John Johnson with him on a visit to the commune this very evening. He went home and showered and built a fire in his office fireplace, working over his desk until his housekeeper brought him his dinner, which he neglected to eat until it was almost cold.

This hero of World War II had spent eleven months in a German prison camp. The experience had been a slice of hell that he wanted to forget, but still he deemed it a small price to pay for the freedom that was proudly and peculiarly American. There was no man or ideology which would arouse his ire so heatedly as the one who would risk bringing the whole country into chains by courting some treachery such as beating machine guns into plowshares in the presence of wicked powers who even now licked their slobbering chops in anticipation of the day when this lovely land would fall.

He shrugged into his jacket and stood for a moment in front of the big window, looking over his fields with introspective melancholy. Long ago he had caught a vision of what it had cost to make this land rich and free, a vision of footprints pressed to the snow—footprints of half-starved soldiers and red-eyed grandpas and hollow-faced virgins and squalling babies; footprints that left little flecks of blood in their wake; footprints leading to the grave so that the world could throw off its chains. He opened the door and went out to the autumn chill spreading across the great spaces, a big man born out of season, keening to winds that had shifted long ago.

At the Kettrie ranch Dow told John, "I'm off to pay my respect to your hippie friends, and I want your company." There had been a time when Dow and John had come close to being comrades, riding and hunting together, drawn by the same discontent over the course of flux that the country seemed to be falling heir to—that is until John's dangerous religion got too much hold on him and he started giving time to every crank and sick coyote that happened along, picking at undisturbed straws, setting in motion a sort of unrest that rubbed against everything from the local school board to the preservation of culture on the Reservation. He never improved anything, Dow often told himself, just asked questions and aroused uneasiness. The influx of hippies was no doubt a deliberate action on John's part to generate more of the tension and upheaval on which he seemed to thrive.

"Someday," he warned as John got into his car beside him, "Somebody's going to shoot you, giving you the martyrdom you want."

John smiled, his eyes touched with sudden humor. "Like a lot of others, you have a high opinion of me, Dow."

"Well, it's clear opinions don't ruffle you; a law unto yourself is what you are."

John sighed. "I'd like to be well thought of, Dow, much as any poor man would like it."

"You ought to be a preacher for bleeding hearts and old ladies. That'd give you the approval you crave and get you off the backs of practical folks."

"Well, now, Dow, you have your faults, too. You're a good rancher but so exclusive folks're afraid to meet you on a common level. Most folks are afraid of you. Ever think of that?"

Dow acted as if he had not heard him and John studied him in the dashboard light. "I told those youngsters to keep the fence up where it joins your place, Dow; haven't they done it?"

"They have to go," Dow replied finally. "I intend to make it plain to them tonight. And if you really have their best interest at heart, you'll back me up. Your barn is gone, maybe an accident, but there could be worse things happen; we have our share of roughnecks that thrive on mischief, especially the kind they can make openly, without fear of reprisal."

John grew quiet and thoughtful. He had his own doubts about the young dreamers finding a meaningful expression in the arid plains, unwitting victims of drift and confusion that they were. They needed a steer in the right direction, and God help him to know what he should do about it. Maybe for their own good they should leave his forty and find some valley where the soil was productive and the mountains hummed with springs. There they could be tucked away from suspicious neighbors. He thought about how the fanatics and their like had their champions only in other lonely souls, detached from the mainstream of society and lodged in dungeons of one sort or another where they were haunted by lost chances at a meaningful destiny. He must be careful not to be moved by his need to identify with the plight of such alienated souls, himself one of them, rather than by a wise regard for their welfare.

As Dow and John drove up, Bobby, his beard still short, sat on the front porch of the new shelter playing his harmonica. "That boy there," John remarked softly, "was in and out of a convalescent hospital twice, but they couldn't cure him of his drug habit."

Dow grunted and got out of the car. "So he's on the weed, eh?"

John gave him a swift look as he fell in stride. "No, he's all right now; this bunch helped him." They walked toward Bobby who was wiping his mouth organ on his shirt and smiling uncertainly at Dow. "Bobby, this is Mr. Garstin," John said. "He wants to meet Brother Rich."

"I've seen you before," Bobby said, shyly, offering his hand. "Everyone here has heard of you, Mr. Garstin."

Dow nodded shortly, ignoring the boy's hand. With agonizing self-awareness, Bobby looked away and started to play the harmonica once more, his long, knotted fingers cupping the instrument tightly.

"Howdy, Brother Rich," John called to the elder brother who was coming toward them from the barn. Grinning broadly, Brother Rich embraced John. "I hope you came to stay the evening."

"'Fraid not, Rich. Mr. Garstin here has to get right along."

"So you're Dow Garstin," Rich gave him an admiring, searching look and held out his hand. "Can't tell you how glad we are to have you here. Come inside and meet some of the others."

Once more Dow ignored the extended hand. "I'm not here as a friendly neighbor," he said softly. "Some Ordlowites were sent by the town hall to ask you to move on, that right?"

"They were here this morning," Rich said quietly.

Dow explained shortly, "I'm here to back them up, to tell you we mean business."

For a minute there was an awkward silence and then Rich inquired, "Can you tell me why you're so dead set on us moving out, Mr. Garstin?"

"We've had bad reports about your beliefs and conduct, that's the first reason. Another thing, you don't know beans about farming, and we can't have your women dying of malnutrition in our backyards. Now I don't intend to talk about it anymore. Just get it all together and leave before winter sets in."

Rich was lost in thought for a minute. When he spoke he seemed to choose his words cautiously. "I understand your concern," he said, "I can appreciate it. If more folks were concerned about protecting their homes, it would be a fine thing." He gazed intently into Dow's face. "But I've heard you're a fair man, Mr. Garstin; that you'd give anybody a hearing, at least once. So I'm asking you to let us defend our reasons for being here." He looked around at sulphurous clouds squatting on the western slopes. "Sundown and it's chilly. Won't you please come inside with me?" He turned and started away as if there was no question but what Dow would follow.

Dow hesitated but already John was going ahead so he went, too, his good sense telling him that he was a fool to let this drag on, his anger mounting as he realized that he had been conned into a sort of momentary compromise by that most artful of all persuasions, an appeal to his ego.

Inside Dow was greeted by a scene that might have been set in the trappings of his early childhood; bundles of hay formed benches against the walls and sheaves of grain hung from the ceiling. Crude tables were being pushed to one end of the room in order to clear the other that was already filling with young people who were seating themselves with a lot of talk and laughter on the straw benches. Dow started to count them, marking off thirty-odd when Rich's voice boomed over their heads. "Soon as we get settled down," he announced, lowering his tone to the sudden, polite quiet, "and now that we're all here"—he looked around, smiling—"I want to introduce a special guest who's with us this evening. Brothers and sisters, this man with our good friend, John Johnson, is our neighbor, Dow Garstin."

A ripple of murmurs passed over the happy faces as they clapped their hands soundly and called out, like children to an offstage cue, "Welcome, Mr. Garstin!"

"Mr. Garstin is a brave and good man, we all know that," Brother Rich went on matter-of-factly. "He's come here because he loves this country and feels responsible for it. He's heard that the town council has told us to leave, and he wants to know if they're justified in doing that. So I asked him to let us acquaint him, at least in a surface way, with our intentions as a family who loves Christ and each other. And he's givin' us this chance."

The room had fallen so quiet that Dow could hear John's breath falling like a sonorous metronome. Blast him for the mischief-maker he was! Dow was sick of the sight of him and all these other gawks and yokels who couldn't make it on the outside. A girl holding a blanketed baby was slowly getting to her feet. "My mother's in a mental hospital," she said, her eyes peering down at her child so it seemed she was talking to it. "She doesn't recognize me when I go to see her. My dad's living with his fourth woman. They don't want me around, never did. These brothers and sisters love me and my baby. They gave me the only home I ever had. I praise God for this—" Her voice broke and she sat down to the comfort of swift hands reaching out to touch her.

The man seated next to her lumbered slowly to his feet, his gaze clinging to Dow's face as he blinked with gentle self-consciousness. "Someday we have to leave this shelter, have to go out into the world and give out the good news of Christ's love. But right now this family is our fold for getting it all together. We're getting fed the Word of life here. We're getting mended where we hurt. It's a work of love, brother, and we thank God every day for it. We thank Him for this big sky, too, and the sun, and the good, clean winds. There's healing in all of it."

As soon as one sat down another stood up. "We're praying day and night for the church of Christ to grow into what God intended for it to be: a servant of the world. Jesus tells us to be givers, not getters. He's been dishonored often enough by Christians who milk the world for all they can get for themselves. They try to justify their greed by claiming God is favoring them because they believe. All of us are just stewards of what the good Lord gives us. We only take what we need, and that's the principle we're trying to live out here."

"We try to be as gentle and meek as doves," a strapping boy with old, twinkly eyes said in a raspy voice. "We don't raise a hand against anyone. Why, man, these hands are the Lord's hands, to be used to comfort and heal."

"I was hooked on hard d-drugs. There was some brain dam-damage. But Jesus is re-restoring my m-mind."

"America's in trouble," one of the girls said from her bench. "We know a lot about the trouble. We came out of it by the power of Jesus Christ. Now we cry out to God to save our nation; we pray for the children who are the real victims of our sins and griefs."

As the testimonials moved on, an all-pervasive sorrow weaved through Dow's innards like the tail of a kite writhing through a soft breeze. He saw that these misguided youngsters were sincere and committed—as he had been committed to old glory and the nation, great and pure. With the logic of a fair man he sought to identify and isolate the force in this place. Somehow his perception had been sharpened so that he detected here a fragment of the stuff and essence of which history was made and the stars also—the same stuff of which these youngsters had caught only a glimpse and were betting that it was everything come together on the head of a pin. But wasn't this the same substance that lured people of terrifying passions to booze, drugs, or false ideas, fastening themselves to the addictions with such gluttonous appetite that they built their sacrificial biers around these iconoclastic chains and surrendered their souls to the hungry blade? He had met dreamers like this before, and they, like kindred spirits everywhere, were guilty of the same romanticism that proved unworkable, even disastrous, in the mainspring of life and reality. Eventually they would give in to disillusionment and failure. And he knew somebody had to be strong enough to free these misguided youths, strong enough to send them home where they just might pick up some good horse sense yet, before their lives were totally rudder-bound.

Finally the last testimonial gave way to an antiphonal chorus—a haunting melody which seemed to clutch at a grief long buried but not quite forgotten. Calling once more on the steel in his marrow to reinforce his mission, he turned and walked out the door.

Anna stood in front of the stained mirror of the bedroom which she shared with Betty, combing her hair with rhythmic strokes. She was glad that her reflection did not betray the restless falling of her heart and the tremulous flutters in her tummy. She felt as if a little sparrow were trapped there. The decision to call on that land baron had been reached last night at the meeting after Dow Garstin left. Elder Brother had said that unless the Lord performed a miracle, they would have to leave this place. At that very moment Anna had been stirred to help the Lord perform such a miracle; and it was such departure from her timid reluctance to get involved in a skirmish that she was convinced the idea was inspired. All night she had lain awake, plotting what she would say to the imposing monarch. Her previously unsolicited encounters had stricken her with awe, but still she was determined to see it through.

A heavy sense of injury made her feel old and sad as she quietly let herself out of the dormitory and slinked out behind the toolshed. Clambering between the barbed wires that let her into the first field of the Garstin ranch, Anna started to run.

Patches of skinny clouds raced overhead as if nature itself was alert to the urgency of Anna's mission. Finally she slowed to a walk, breathing, struggling for gulps of crisp, autumn air. "Help me, Lord, to speak your words and not my own." Her prayer was lifted skyward by a driving wind that seemed to come from nowhere, sending tumbleweeds scurrying like fat old ladies running to market. Overhead the scattered clouds had drawn together to form a leaden blanket and soon it started to rain—big, erratic drops of sleet that pelted the dusty trail like white daubs of paint being sucked up by old canvas.

As the storm grew in severity Anna's conviction about her errand wavered; it seemed now that even heaven was conspiring against her. She shivered in the cold deluge that was now rain, now snow. Hadn't elder brother warned them all that once they had received the witness in their spirit about a matter, hell itself should not swerve them from obedience? Holding her side against a throbbing pain she went on.

She arrived at the back door of the big ranch house, shivering and fairly exhausted, laboring to maintain her resolve by summoning memories from her past—memories of sadness in which she had always known that her parents' house had needed a certain quality of joy to make it a real home, just like this proud baron needed to learn to like poor and ignorant people in order for this great house to be a home.

When the door did not open to her repeated knockings, she moved around to the back. From within she could hear the urgent barking of dogs. Suddenly the rear door opened. Before her stood the one whom her soul both dreaded and fastened upon. "Girl," he cried, "what the devil are you doing out here in the rain!"

Disadvantaged by his towering figure, Anna felt the trapped sparrow in her tummy try its wings over and over. When she finally found her voice, it was a shrill and hateful thing which she would rather not have claimed. "I've come for the good of your soul!" She shrieked with the discord of the rejected, despising herself for being such a miserable representative of His saving grace.

"Come in, young lady," the baron ordered. "We'll see you get dried off and returned to your home!"

She shook her head, swallowing a large raindrop before she got her larynx working again. "I only came to give you a message! I can't come in. I want nothing from you. . . . "

"I can't understand a word you're saying! Come in before you float away."

Her legs moving like bellows of sponge toward him, Anna went on with her speech, "I'm here to tell you about *yourself*, Mr. Garstin. Probably nobody in your whole life has helped you take a good look at *yourself*. . . . "

"Mrs. Heath!" Dow called out to someone bustling in another room. "Come give us a hand here!" He gave Anna's arm a little tug and shut the door behind her. "Now who are you, young lady? Are you lost?"

"I'm one of the helpers at the commune that you ordered off John's land; but before we leave, we owe it to you to tell you how selfish and cruel and unfeeling you really are. Yes, we owe you that for the good of your eternal soul. Maybe in the world to come you, too, will be poor and helpless. Then you will know how it feels to be treated like dirt. All we want is to make this world a better place!" Her words were falling from her lips like fragments of yarn all balled up in a messy wad, and a frightening thing it was with Dow Garstin surveying her with eyes cold and narrowed.

"Ah," Dow nodded as understanding settled in, his expression softening. "So you want to save the world, you say?"

Anna hung her head, suspicious of the mocking yet kindly quality of his manner.

"Well, young lady, the best way you and your friends can accomplish that is for each one of you to go home, get jobs, go to school, elect decent men to office, build something sound for your own children."

Anna pushed nervously at her limp, wet hair. "Not all of us are strong enough to do that yet, but we will in time, you'll see. Most of our people do not have homes to return to. They're hurting deep inside; they've been wounded by the poisons and confusions of our times. This is why we open our hearts and doors to the riffraff, as you regard them; they're helpless, they're messed up. They haven't had tidy upbringings like your Montana farm boys. They don't know who to turn to or where to go. They're looking for a reason to live."

"I don't doubt your sincerity, young lady, or what you're trying to say about human need. But most of you youngsters want a free ride and, by George, I won't give one to the yokel healthy enough to pay his own fare." When Anna replied that most of them were not healthy, mentally or emotionally, that was just the problem, Dow went right on talking, drowning out the sound of her voice. "I'll go the added mile for a good man who wants to better his lot with responsible work, but I'll be laid end to end before I'll bend over and play rich uncle for a pack of beggars who'd reduce me to their own level the next round!"

"It's your glorious society that's made poor, helpless children out of them."

"Don't blame it on me. I'm not responsible, not in the remotest."

Anna sighed. "You sound like a good churchman. The church

won't assume responsibility, either, not until we can all sing 'Faith of Our Fathers' with clean coats and plastic faces."

"It's nothing to me that you feel too good for the church," Dow told her. "I've given it too wide a berth to be burned by it." He went on, as if musing to himself. "But it's been a friend to the sick and poor in the past, as far as I can see, helping to protect the community from certain ills. Their problem now is the rabble moving in on them, playing along with the political tune of communists and their bedfellows."

"We take the words of Jesus concerning self-denial very seriously, sharing what we have with the poor and sick; we're very happy living this Word of love."

"If you're so happy, why don't you join the churches and live it there?" Dow shrugged impatiently.

"We can't have any part in bearing arms, and most churches have a problem handling that."

"Thank God for that or we'd all be in trouble," Dow snapped irritably.

"If God's people will be faithful to live for Him and trust Him, He'll put an end to violence and killing."

Dow looked at her in amazement and disgust. "This is a lot of nonsense talk; I have chores to do."

"People need to listen to each other," Anna said softly.

"You've had your say."

Anna wrung her hands with helpless tension. "How rude you are. I wanted you to understand."

"Afraid I do," he said coldly.

"No, you really don't, but I guess you can't help it. You're too old and stubborn," she added sadly.

"Mrs. Heath will help you find your way home," he said curtly, dismissing her and leaving her to stand in a puddle of water that had drained from her clothes while he went out into the hallway.

"Never mind," Anna whispered, "I'm not afraid." Quietly she turned and let herself out. The malicious wind bit through her wet clothing as Dow Garstin's voice echoed in her ears, "Mrs. Heath, are you deaf? Come help me here. . . ."

Anna raced into the gathering gloom. The field grass was wet and sharp, and she quickly found a shallow place in the ditch where she could cross onto the county road. With the wind to her back and her hair flying around her face like witches' tails and the exertion of her anxiety causing a feeling akin to levitation, she thought about how it would feel to die and have your spirit soar up, up to worlds beyond. And then she thought about how Enoch and Elijah had been translated and she wondered if Moses, too, had been translated, because nobody had ever found his body and he had gone alone up the mountain at the Lord's request when it was time for him to die. Just now her thoughts were all jumbled together with her own desire to leave the world and float straight into the arms of Jesus. Suddenly the headlights of a car came in behind her, startling her so that she spun around and froze to the side of the road.

"Aren't you a long way from home?" It was Kip Kettrie. His smile and warmth so relieved Anna and filled her to the brim with such glad longings that she was already fumbling with the door handle when he said, "Well, what're you waiting for? Scared to ride with me?" She quickly returned his smile as she climbed into the pickup seat beside him, still trembling from her unsuccessful meeting with Dow Garstin.

Right away Kip started asking her questions. He was so warm and friendly she could not take offense. And yet he made her slightly uncomfortable. "Where's your hometown?" he asked first.

"Seattle."

"Must seem pretty quiet around here."

"I like the quiet."

"You're happy, then?"

"Yes."

"Well, I'm awfully curious as to why a pretty, smart girl like yourself is living in a religious commune in the middle of nowhere."

"I wasn't always so smart—nor pretty, either."

"Well, now that you are, what are you doing here?"

"Maybe I'm trying to be of some use," she said. "The Community of Helpers is my family. We love each other."

"Ummm. Couldn't you get the same kind of support in some church? John's your friend and he helps people through his church. So do most other Christians; they help each other, they reach out to their neighbors."

Anna chewed at her lip. There it was again, a word she was starting to hate. She was sick of hearing about *church*! And Kip's quick observation had not been lost on her. He had thought this through before.

"And isn't it tough living *all huddled* together," he went on, "not having your own place or privacy?"

She hesitated and looked hard at a little spot on the windshield. "Of course it's hard sometimes. My roommate has trouble with her adenoids so she snores and keeps me awake. I get mashed up about it sometimes." She thought about one night when Annabelle Lee had filled the room with her sonorous wheezing. Anna had grown so frustrated that little rivers of crawlies had crept under her skin, making her want to scream; and she had rolled out of bed and pinched Annabelle Lee and told her to turn over and shut her mouth—which the poor girl had done with such humility that Anna had been thoroughly ashamed and had apologized over and over the next day. "But who said life is supposed to be easy street? Besides, I love my roommate. Annabelle Lee's her name, and I know she's in the right place for the healing of the scars in her mind. She was a slave, you know, locked in a room of a house owned by a devil who sold her body to anyone off the street. She'd still be there if Brother Ben hadn't led someone to his own place who told him about this girl. Ben rescued her," she added proudly, "and that devil is in jail. The hardest thing any of us ever did was to learn to pray for him with compassion."

Kip was plainly shocked by her story. "Man, I've heard of such things. . . " he muttered in wonder.

Outside a few lonely snowflakes went helterskelter across the headlights. Anna nodded sadly. "She was a runaway. They're everywhere these days—poor, dumb kids—thanks to messed-up homes and wrong choices. It doesn't take long to ruin children, but it takes God a while to bring them back to normal. He can't do it without some of us willing to be the vessels of His healing love."

Kip was thoughtful. A sense of respect made him very polite and quiet. How sheltered he and others like him were in this big country, far removed from the grotesque shapes to which Anna was giving flesh and form.

Anna grew pensive. Talking about Annabelle's past depressed her as imaginings of the most evil sort leaped across her brain like electricity skittering across live wires. Such a melancholy sorrow set in that she wanted to take off and hide herself in some out-of-the-way spot where she could weep and moan and try to give back to God His burden for a world that was shot through with little black holes full of unspeakable sufferings and sadistic demons. "Whatever is pure and lovely, think on these things," Brother Rich often read from the Word. But at times the desperate condition of the brothers and sisters coming for help caused them all to cry out to God for them and others still out there, away from the fold, far from the tender Father's care. "Oh, bring the prodigal home," they sighed; "Bring the world to Jesus." She sighed now, bringing her thoughts back to Kip and giving in to the pleasure of his company. What a beautiful man he is, she thought, aware that her prayers on his behalf had made him very close to her somehow even though an unapproachable chasm lay between them—the chasm of her unworthiness and his worldliness.

Kip was steering the pickup close to the vestibule of the old schoolhouse where the headlights exposed the sign over the door: COMMUNITY OF HELPERS. He went around and assisted Anna from the rig, his touch causing her to draw back. "You're plumb different," he said, grinning , as if that were a plus for her, "and I think I like what you're doing to save the world."

Anna's heart began pounding with joy. She wanted to say something that would let him know how fine he was. "God bless you," she blurted, darting inside the lighted cove of the porch and not even turning her head when he called out, "Hey, what's your name?" Just his wanting to know her name set her to trembling with pleasure, making her suddenly shy and mysterious so that she slammed the door swiftly behind her, as if she had not heard him calling.

Inside, some of the brothers and sisters had a prayer vigil going, beseeching the Lord to keep them in this place. "Winter's coming on," one of them was saying from the edge of the circle, "winter's coming on and we have no place to go. Protect us, Lord; give us favor in the eyes of the good people of Ordlow County."

Anna summoned her emotions back from their romantic journey to join the prayer ring. "My dear precious Father," she whispered, "I may never have a husband, but I have you. I love you with all my being." As she worshipped Him, the sense of His presence made her cry with joy and thanksgiving.

After a while Brother Rich said, "We are committed to the gentle peace of Jesus, brothers and sisters. There'll be no violence on account of us. Now we will prove our God. He will tell us what to do. He will protect us, unworthy servants though we are. Our eyes are on Him." They sang then, their praises lifting the rafters of the old schoolhouse and setting the coyotes to howling. "Stand still and see the salvation of our God," Brother Ben proclaimed, his face shining with love. They all answered, "Amen." And then they went to their beds, full of peace and trust.

Anna fell into such a deep slumber that when she felt someone shaking her by the arm, it seemed she had been sleeping for hours.

"Shhh," Betty hissed. "Don't make a sound. I'm scared. There's at least two men out in the cornfield. I heard a voice."

Suddenly Anna was wide awake and ready for whatever. "C'mere," Betty was urging, her hand still clutching tightly to Anna's arm, "and look out the window."

It was a black night. The slivered moon gave off only a sullen halo through the blankets of cloud. The silhouettes of the straggling cornstalks were barely discernible. "I don't see a thing," Anna said, almost petulantly. "You're getting paranoid, Betty."

Just then a shot rang out, hitting the stillness like an explosion. Anna gasped and pulled Betty away from the window. Now Annabelle Lee was awake and frightened, also. Betty ran to the next space to get her baby and returned a moment later, cradling him in her arms.

"What's going on!" Annabelle Lee demanded.

"Shhh," Betty said, as Annabelle, too, slipped out from her covers and came to stand in front of the window, pushing her face in close just above Betty.

"I seem to *sense* movement more than I can *see* it—over there in the barrow pit," Anna murmured, pushing the window up a crack.

"Ohhh," Betty started weeping, "Jesus, help us."

"Hush your crying," Anna said sternly. "Our Lord is here; nothing can hurt us." All three stood as still as stone, hardly breathing. After a little while Anna was certain she heard someone use the name "Clint," and she started to tremble nervously. "It's that same bunch who dumped our potatoes," she whispered. "It's them, I know it!"

"We *prayed* for them," Betty said accusingly.

"Be QUIET, Betty!" Anna snapped, suddenly angry.

Just then the yard light came on and Brother Ben came out and stood in the bright glare. Anna was thinking about how skinny and alone he looked when Rich ran out to stand beside him. "We are unarmed, friends," Ben called out, his voice slicing the stillness like a trumpet. "Come out and show yourselves."

Another shot rang out and it seemed to whistle right over Ben's head.

"They'll kill him!" Annabelle Lee started to cry. "They'll kill Brother Ben. I always knew he had the gift of martyrdom. I knew it!"

"Just pray and be quiet!" Anna commanded, her own nerves as jittery as a cat's in a barrel.

At that moment a scream rent the air, followed by silhouettes climbing the far bank of the barrow pit and running into the dark. A terrible stench of skunk wasted through the crack in the dormitory window. "Skunk!" someone shouted in the distance. Now Anna could count six men running down the road, and in a few minutes a car coughed and started wheeling on the highway toward town. "Wait, wait for me—" someone was calling hoarsely, and Anna could make out a lone figure racing after the retreating car.

Into the startled silence came the brothers and sisters, some of them cracking up with laughter, others shouting their praises to the sky. Very soon, in that cold, dark pre-dawn under the yard light, they started dancing and singing. "Though a host camp against me/the Lord, my God protects me/He is my deliverer/none shall make me afraid." Oblivious to the terrible odor of skunk oil, they sang praises and danced, and then they went back to bed and slept the sound sleep of the loved and cradled.

The next morning Brother Ben shared with them all what the Lord had put on his heart to do. He would go to Father Stewart and Pastor Greene and ask them to help some of the brothers get work with the new rest home. "Only we will work as unpaid servants; we will win these people through our love and humble service. Brothers and sisters, stand still and see the salvation of the Lord!"

6

Winter Storm

It is snowtime and my crippled darlin'
limps a path for me,
through whirling down and silver wind. . . .

COLD WEATHER fell like a whiplash across the range. Kip skated over the wandering ribbon of frozen creek. Sometimes he brought a friend to stay the night and they would skate by the unshapely flames of a bonfire in the inlet until they were wet and numb with cold, making their way back to the house where Urliss fed them steaming bowls of chowder and muffins and strong black coffee.

Then the snows moved in, hard and driving. The bedroom windows upstairs became networks of frozen lace, and Kip would defrost a peephole by smudging his breath on one spot and drying it with his handkerchief so that he could see the ranch glittering under its ocean of winter covers. When the cows picked their way in to drink at the corral, their breath rose like steam, their hooves snapped the crusty snow like branches falling.

With the holidays coming on, Urliss was in turn self-important and distracted. She was plotting an old-fashioned Christmas replete with streamers of hearts and homemade candles and bells that would hang near the entrance where the chimes could pipe and warble and take the mourning off the wind.

Every Saturday Kip took her to town to shop. Although she pretended it was a tiring chore, secretly she was pleased to while away the hours scrutinizing each store's merchandise with endless deliberation, only rarely making a purchase, such as the material from which to make a little *Yule nisse* like the one which had guarded her childhood home in Norway.

One afternoon Kip arrived home from school earlier than usual to find Urliss fluttering excitedly over a special candle mold that the day's mail had delivered, wondering if it would be too much to ask him to take her into town for another square of wax so she could set the candle next morning. "For Pete's sake, Urliss," Kip was annoyed with what he considered a presumption on her part, "I just came from town. I've got a dozen chores to do!" But observing her disappointment he agreed to take her after all, with the understanding that she would pick up what she needed and they would get right back home again.

In Ordlow the snow fell softly on the intersection where a spruce tree rose like a blinking maypole and high cobwebs of lights weaved in and out between the lamp posts. Everywhere the carols sounded over jarring speakers, and the festive spirit worked like fever in her veins as Urliss hugged her elation and plodded up and down the streets.

Drifting through the notions and hardware aisles, she admired the decorations. Spying a gold and ivory porcelain angel, she considered buying it for the buffet, hovered over it, fingered it lovingly, went away, returned several times to see if it was still there and finally snatched it up quickly lest she change her mind.

A heartwarming time it was, tracking in and out of the shops, beaming greetings at every familiar face. She spied Mrs. Garrett behind a kitchenware rack, her small berry eyes squinting and snapping, her lips—like her skin—paper dry and slightly yellow, rubbing together as she mumbled to herself. Mrs. Garrett did not like Urliss and the feeling was mutual, but in her generous mood Urliss called out, "All set for the holidays, Mrs. Garrett?"

"—ready before Thanksgivin'," she mumbled through fretting lips, and Urliss was suddenly uneasy as if someone had stepped on her grave. The clock in the dry-goods section said seven-fifteen. Full dark had set in long ago, and she ran to the department store where she picked up her block of wax.

Arriving back at the truck, she waved apologetically at Kip who was pacing up and down the street, hunched into his jacket, his breath a ragged mist, his nose and ears beet red. "Ah, Kipper, I am late but it took so long," she shrugged vaguely; "maybe ve should catch some soup."

With chin stuffed into his collar Kip smiled tightly and shook his head as he opened the pickup door for Urliss while tossing the wax into the truck bed. "The wind's coming up, Urliss, throwin' that snow around. We can come in again Saturday and have lunch with Mrs. Brennan." He backed cautiously into the street.

Sighing inwardly, Urliss agreed and thought once more how she would like to live right in this town with its friendly people hallooing and smiling at you, imagining how it would feel to be clerking at Myerson's, selling coats and dresses to the ladies. *"No, no, dis suit vill not do—too drab. You need bright color and soft line, see! Dis is lovely, yust lovely, and scarf to match, a touch at neck like so. . . ."*

The chains clanked and frumped over the highway until they turned onto the big flat where they bit into packed snow. Now the flakes were swirling hypnotically into the headlights. Urliss unwrapped her Christmas *engel* and held it under the steering wheel so the dash light could play on the gold-etched wings. "Can you see dis, Kipper?"

"Very pretty," he said, smiling.

"For de buffet; ah, vill be a fine Christmas, I promise."

Kip desperately hung onto his smile, while images of past Christmases flew at him. Mentally he tried to unwrap the memory of his father puffing through a great cotton beard and his mother tickling him awake in the cold upstairs bedroom while warm oven smells crawled through the register. But the spirit of those festive times seemed to slip through his grasp, leaving only the bittersweet of that which was gone forever. The cab was warm now and the heater fan hummed noisily. A high wind came leaping from all directions and Kip dropped the speed.

"I glad you do de driving, Kipper," Urliss acknowledged thankfully. "Ven I drive in Norvay, ve never have veder so bad in vinter."

Urliss went on with her planning of the Yuletide celebration from breakfast to the last ember. Ethan had spent Thanksgiving with his girlfriend's family in Minneapolis, but he would be home for the holidays; and Urliss must see to it that all things were done well so that the three of them would keep a good memory of this time instead of being haunted by old griefs and missing pieces.

Suddenly she realized that the pickup was barely crawling,

and her attention was riveted to the road ahead where the wind was blowing the powdered snow into great, blinding funnels that rose to meet the dense blanket falling from the sky. In the dim light of the cab she saw that Kip's face was masked with tension. Fear set her heart to pounding. "Oh, Kip," she whispered.

He rolled the window down and stuck his head out into the lash of the wicked blizzard, steering by spastic glimpses of the road edge. Coming to the turn at the top of the hill he completely lost visibility and plowed into a massive snowbank left by the country grader on its weekly round. Shifting into reverse he twisted the wheel, racing and depressing the accelerator, trying to back out, straining to extricate the rig for long, awful minutes. "Curse me for the dumb buzzard I am," he ranted. "I should have turned back miles ago!"

Urliss could not speak, terror throbbed in her temples and squeezed at her throat. A deep foreboding crouched like a devil on her brain.

"We'll have to wait it out, Urliss," Kip said, finally, his tone of voice firm with what he hoped was reassurance. "We'll just hope the storm lets up and somebody as stupid as I am comes by."

"Maybe John vill come?"

"Maybe." But Kip knew the storm warnings must have been out hours ago, and John would expect them to sit tight wherever they were. No doubt the phones were out so John would have no way of checking even if he tried. Still, he might tackle the road for a ways. They could play with that hope.

The gas tank was over half full so they could keep the motor running and the heater turned on. Kip lowered his window a crack for safety. Snow started gathering on the windshield like little mounds of cotton. "Let's sing some carols," Kip suggested, "it'll help pass the time. And Urliss," he added kindly, "we might spend a cramped, uncomfortable night, but the storm is bound to blow itself out so don't be afraid."

Urliss thought about that for a little while and then she started to sing "*Glade jul, hellige jul*—Silent night, holy night," in a hopeful, thin, wavering voice that grew stronger and more natural as she moved into the song. Kip followed her in a lower octave and they went on to decking the halls and a partridge in a pear tree and then Urliss sang "*Hvad barn er det*—What child is this who laid to rest—" and Kip listened carefully because he did not know it, listened and was overcome with heavy feelings. The impression of a mysterious babe at a mother's breast stirred his own longings for the familiar hearth and his mother and the fields in the new spring with the first pale fringe of grain tickling the air and the birds peeping at the luminous pearls of wind and sky. All of this quickened his inner spirit to recognize the profound and common experience of life offered to every child birthed to life's lashing storm and a mother's breast. Kip joined her again and they sang on until they had run the gamut of known carols; and then they sat listening to the tumult outside, listening to the crashing and screaming going on all around them.

The glowing hands of Kip's watch said ten-thirty. Already it seemed they had entered the first gate of eternity. When he turned off the ignition a fog of bitter air soon enough seeped through the floor and their feet grew cold. They shivered through their coats, so once again he turned the motor on. The warmth of their confined shelter and the roar of the storm was beginning to make them drowsy. Time and again a creeping somnolence settled over Kip, and he would fight to shake himself loose from that soft, sweet cradle; but once he failed to rouse and soon he was breathing evenly.

The next thing he knew Urliss was shaking him. "Kipper, turn de heat on. Qvick! I ache from cold!" She chattered and shivered in her urgency.

Kip lurched for the key, turning it as he pressed his foot on the gas. The only response he got was a faint groan in the motor. He felt himself on the verge of panic. How long had the heater fan run after the engine died? He couldn't tell, but one thing was for sure: the battery was dead. His mind groped feverishly. He looked hard at his watch. Two o'clock! His sheltered side of the pickup was buried under a thick white frosting and a mound of snow fell into his lap as he rolled the window down part way. The wind slapped at him with pelting flakes.

"Listen, Urliss, listen now," he said, sorting his thoughts aloud. "I know better than to move into a blizzard, but if we stay here we'll freeze. About two, maybe three miles up the road there's a shack where John used to stay when we ran sheep. My mother kept it up more or less for harvesters when they worked the south fields. We can follow the fence till we reach the gate. I know it's risky, but I think we can make it."

Reaching behind the seat he groped around until he found a ragged blanket which he tore into long strips, Urliss watching terror-stricken. "Tie one of these around your face and another over your forehead, then bind what you can around your legs." He wound a strip around his own face and pulled his cap down over his forehead so that only his eyes were visible. "After we start walking don't try to talk unless you absolutely have to. Save your breath."

He pushed himself out the door and held it open for Urliss. Still clutching her Christmas angel, she followed him to the ditch where they broke crust and floundered in snow up to their hips. They crawled up the bank and helped each other through the barb wire fence, staying close to it as they moved on. They were heading into the gate now, bowing their heads to the driving spray, with Kip swathing a path for Urliss to follow.

Kip rammed into a fence post before he realized they had come to the end of the field. Still clinging to the wire he turned sharply to the right. He had two worries: first, that they would give up before they ever reached the cabin and, next, that the gate leading from the main road to the cabin's trail would be shut if they did make it. If that gate were closed he would mistake it for fence and go right on toward miles of open land.

Urliss's breath was coming in tearing sobs. Time and again they stopped and Kip put his arms around her, trying to protect her with his long, lanky body as they stood with their backs to the wind, trying to rest. Finally they stumbled on, the ragged scarves over their mouths turning to thick, frozen slush, their feet lashed with pain and, eventually, numb as stone.

The first time Urliss fell she made little sound and Kip only instinctively turned and pulled her up. She clung to him as he yelled, "Walk! Walk!" the wind swallowing his desperate command.

"Rest. I must rest." The words barely escaped her paralyzed lips. Kip grabbed her with one arm, feeling for the fence with the other. Staggering on, they hadn't gone more than twenty yards until Urliss fell agan. Once more Kip coaxed her to her feet.

Hear that wind, Urliss thought. Hear it now. It was the land calling for her—big, hungry land, calling for the last ounce of flesh, for the torn sinews of her mind, calling for heroics from dead bones. *Herre Gud*, hear it now.

Biting and shrieking its fury, the wind called *Urlissssss.* . . . She tightened her hold on the little angel, unable to feel her arms pressing, wondering at the little push against her chest. Would her ears never stop ringing? Think of a number then; oh, think—seven. Yes, it was a good number, see what it brought: a warm puff of summer, calling low like a little moan in the meadow. "How soft de grass vas, so soft," she murmured. "Rest vill be sveet, only hush de vind, hush now. . . ."

Kip staggered on like a robot, his own body so heavy that he had not even noticed when Urliss fell for the last time. His breath came in great, rending sobs, his feet were iron weights, his eyelids heavy casts of ice. When he ran out of fence he was too exhausted to feel excited. This, then, was the gate. He moved straight ahead until he came to the next fence post and retraced his steps. Yes, this was the gate. He hung onto the first post as bellows of fire pounded at his mind and illumined his raw lungs. He forced his eyes to peer obliquely through the hurtling snow.

"*Urliss!*" Her name was only a flame in his mind, but he thought he had shouted it to the sky. *Urliss!*" He stumbled back now, back along the fence, feeling with an outstretched leg for the lump of her fallen body. When he found her, he was afraid to kneel down for fear he would not get up so he nudged her with his boot. She was motionless. Unconscious, he thought, or dead.

Clinging to another fence post, he tried to work his way through the spots and clouds in his mind. If Urliss was dead he had killed her, better for him to go to sleep beside her. God, if you really exist, help me, help her.

Struggling to muster strength from somewhere, he leaned over Urliss until he had a grip on her coat and started dragging her by spurts and inches until they were back at the gate. Now he must move straight to the right; if he veered off course he would miss the cabin.

His chest was exploding into bits and pieces, his throat felt as if it was torn and bleeding. Urliss was unbelievably heavy; he could not carry her. He pulled her on through the snow, step by brutal step, forever and ever. He stumbled and fell and lay unmoving, until a dim message floated on his weary brain: he had stumbled on the pump block; the cabin was here.

Crawling to the left he glimpsed a solid rectangle gaping from the swirling snow. With his teeth he pulled off a frozen glove and commanded his body to stand erect one last time. Then he unlatched the door and went back for Urliss, pulling her with clumsy, erratic movements until they were inside the cabin. Useless to try to get her up onto the bed, he grabbed quilts from the mattress and threw them over her and lay down beside her.

Heaving coals of fire from his lungs, he felt himself falling away, away, growing smaller and smaller.

He awakened to the sounds of wailing. For a long time he could not remember where he was; and when memory came, disbelief and horror followed.

Now the sun filtered through the little frozen window, the air was crisp and cold.

But the wailing was real. Urliss had made a fire in the stove and was writhing on the bed, holding one hand pathetically inside the other and then tenderly shifting their positions.

"Urliss," his voice cracked, "what is—?" And then it came to him. She was thawing out, and all her fingers and joints were crying their abuse; there was no more tender pain than this. But she was alive. He curled up tighter in the quilt and slept again.

7

Melanie

Like lonesome children the old ghosts come
When Christmas bells sound across the field,
Calling hidden playmates from where they crouch
In the wistful crags of my recollections. . . .

FOR URLISS, whose devotion to Kip had bordered on single-minded intensity in the past, the storm experience heightened her admiration so that she could not do enough for him. The thought that she owed him her very breath dominated her waking moments and called her to a slavish concern for his comfort—a concern which wore them both out as she "cooked the dish Kip like" and smothered him with fluttering attentions that included polishing his shoes and cleaning his razor. She never thought to analyze these feelings, whether they were motherly yearnings or the infatuation of an unloved spinster.

Finally Kip grew embarrassed, then indignant. "Urliss, for Pete's sake, relax, will you?" He laughed weakly. "You're treating me like I'm missing a head."

She stared hard at him and turned away, back to her soup making.

"It's not that I'm ungrateful, Urliss," he hastened to add, "but you're making me squirm."

She sighed and then laughed. Her face went soft at his discomfiture; hands poised mid-air above her noodle mix, while her eyes sparkled, she shot back, "Okay, tomorrow I sleep in; you get breakfast."

From that time on their friendship settled into a sort of bedrock, undisturbed by their shifting moods. "He is my engel boy, dat vun," Urliss would murmur. Her thoughts were forever call-

ing his gentle, softly planed face with its cowl of dark hair to re-
membrance. One time she would be cooing over him with all the
charm of a mother's tenderness; the next she'd be softly scolding,
reprimanding him about things that really didn't bother her but
nevertheless afforded her the opportunity to pay attention to
him. He accepted her mothering with good-natured grace.

With Christmas only ten days away they received word that
Ethan was bringing his girlfriend home for the holidays. The
news, coming through a letter to Kip, was unsettling to Urliss.
She grew annoyed thinking about all the extra fuss and bother
this would make for her. It would mean stripping the main bedroom and waxing it down, and she would have to arrange enter-
tainment and bite her tongue and act the hostess, all of which
would contribute to a sense of uneasiness that would alienate her
from the boys. No, she did not like it. "Tell Etan be sure de girl
has parents' permission," she told Kip when he was starting to
frame a reply. "Tell him I like to hear from her muder," she added primly, pleased that she should think of it. "If her muder not
write, she stay home; tell him dis."

Kip agreed patiently. "I'm sure she has the green light from
home, but I'll remind him."

"Remember de letter from de muder," Urliss repeated, enjoying a sly feeling of power. "No letter, no . . . vat's her name?"

"Melanie." Kip rolled the word around his tongue. "Pretty
name."

"Yah, no letter, no Melanie."

"He likes her," Kip mused, "really likes her. I wonder if he's
serious, if they'll end up getting married?"

Urliss shrugged. "He's a baby yet."

"Uncle George married young; Ethan might, too."

So her name was Melanie, from Minneapolis. Urliss envis-
aged a vain, lazy city girl, tormenting the substance out of her
own carefully planned holidays and wavered between resentment
and a quiescent pride in her competence as mistress of Shellydown. But she was sure she could handle the situation gra-
ciously.

Urliss was thinking ahead, to games by the fireplace while
they ate popcorn and creme candies—games like Scrabble, or
checkers or maybe pinocle—that is, if a southerly wind didn't
smoke them out of the room.

On the day before Christmas Kip did the choring and feeding under a sky plastered with frozen clouds all curdled up like clabbered milk. He had a certain habit of smiling to himself when he was pleased and often the smile fell into a wide grin that lit his face like a candle. Right now he was pleased, so he went about his chores with a brightness that shed a little extra favor even on the animals.

Trudging through the snow, he stopped to rub the horses' heads as they came up to drink. The windmill pump screeched as the piston fought up and down and water gushed into the tank. *Ethan is coming home.* When John came on the scene, he called, "John, did I tell you Ethan is coming today?"

"Someone told me," John said, grinning.

"Do you know he's already qualified for a scholarship?"

"I'm not surprised. He has a good head."

"Everyone knows he's got it all together. He could be president if he cared to. Did you know he's majoring in law? Yep, he sure could be president someday."

John thought about that. "Like we said, he's smart; he wouldn't want the job."

"Well, we might have to settle for Senator." He took off for the house, quivering with nervous expectancy. Any minute now Ethan's Ford would gun around the bend. He cleaned his room and showered and roamed in and out of the kitchen where Urliss was bustling and murmuring over the stove.

The kitchen was a big, light room with a winter range and a long oval table. Here amidst plates and elbows, the Kettrie family history had been shaped while they slumped into caned chairs, cradling mugs of steaming coffee and sharing their hopes and regrets.

Through the tangle of plants all crowded into the corner window for light, Kip picked out a view of the road, the little smile on his lips coming and going as he thought about how it would be when he and his brother saw each other. He wondered how they would look and what they would say. Kip supposed that Ethan's girlfriend would give Urliss a hand in the kitchen now and then so he and Ethan would be free to spar off like they wanted. And then there would be those late night hours when they went upstairs to turn in and they could hash over all that had been happening in each of their lives. Maybe they'd even talk about how they felt now since their folks were gone forever—whether at times they still stuffed their faces hard against their pillows to keep their sounds inside.

Urliss was cutting bread for the dressing, cleaving the big knife over the board with methodical strokes. For a long time she had wanted to tell Kip something of her own mother and now, while he sat captive at the table, seemed as good a time as any.

"Mine vas—vat you say—eart' muder," she began, "strong vid a big lap to hold all us little vuns at same time. Yah, a big lap and a heart of many passions; she vun time fight a bear for my bruder."

Nodding at the sudden interest in Kip's expression, she continued with great feeling. "De bear caught my bruder and carry him off and my muder ran after and fought de bear vid a club and saved my bruder vid only his arm tore off."

A horn blared in the distance. "Ethan!" Kip ran out the door. Urliss sighed and went on remembering the past. "She could not scream at de bear, my muder; she vas deef and dumb. Deef and dumb. On Christmas Eve ve sing *Glade Jul*, my bruders and fader and uncles and me, but my muder's hands sing best of all. . . ."

Kip planted his feet and grinned while the car tore up the lane, Ethan still camping on the horn; and when the car came to an abrupt halt and Ethan jumped out, the brothers hugged and hit each other like playful cubs.

"Your hair is long enough for pigtails," Kip observed, "wait'll Dow gets a load of that!"

"And you're still a skinny weakling; too bad you can't have my starchy dorm dinners." He slapped his stomach.

"Yeah, that's a lot o' lard all right. . . ." Kip's attention swerved to the other side of the car where a girl had emerged and was edging toward them.

"Hey," Ethan murmured, reaching over to take her hand and draw her to himself, "Melanie, this is Kip. Kip, meet my girl." His eyes glowed with pride.

Exquisitely fine-boned, she might have been dipped in honey and roses and dried under a new sun on a misty morning. Kip looked fully at her and felt the breath swoosh right out of him. He took the delicate hand that she slipped into his own and held it as if he were afraid it might break. Her eyes were deep blue, almost violet, and when she smiled she caught the top edge of her lower lip with even white teeth. "You're exactly like I thought you'd be from all Ethan told me," she said in a voice that tinkled like wind chimes in the softest stirring air.

Ethan raised his brows. "If I'd told you everything, you'd have been scared to come. He walks in his sleep, has fits after dinner. . . ."

Kip was shy and deliriously happy at the same time. With tongue-tied courtesy he steered them to the house where pungent aromas of pine and cloves and orange and scented candles jogged their senses to a deeper appreciation of the decor that splashed extravagantly through the rooms, like daubs on an easel. Urliss met them with a dignified reserve that dissolved quickly under Melanie's ecstasy over her handiwork. "Oh, it is charming!" she exclaimed, clapping her hands as she examined each heart and bell and candle. "I'm so happy to be here, so happy!" she chirped like a merry bird.

With a composure born of a reaffirmed self-respect, Urliss served them hot spicy cider from old tea cups. It was plain that she, too, was favorably impressed with this amiable girl who had snatched Ethan up into some light-headed realm that Urliss recalled experiencing herself in a past crush or fancy.

There was a contagion about Melanie's spirit, Kip decided, that suffused the room with tenderness, putting everyone at ease and making them all seem witty and charming, even to themselves. In the next hour he learned that Melanie's father was a druggist, her mother a pediatrician, and she was an only child.

"She plays the violin," Ethan announced, "and her major is political science. I think she wants to be governor."

"She might get, I tink," Urliss said.

"I'm much too lazy," Melanie laughed. "I'd rather catch a rich husband and run for chairman of Feminists, Inc."

"If you get a husband who's good-lookin', strong, and counts to fifty-five without stuttering," Ethan instructed her, "that's enough; you just plan on running for governor."

She giggled. "If you say so," she smiled up at him and twined her fingers through his. Very carefully Ethan planted a kiss on the tip of her nose.

Watching them aroused little cat's paws of aches and fevers in Kip. His admiration for his brother's taste in girls was boundless at this moment, and he wondered how he had ever found Melanie. And then it came to him: Ethan deserved the very best there was, and some tide in the affairs of law and fortune had seen to it that he got it.

After dinner Kip and Ethan unloaded suitcases from the car and put Melanie's things in the bedroom that had belonged to their parents. Then they sat at the kitchen table while Melanie dried dishes for Urliss. Weighing his words cautiously, Kip put the burden of conversation on his brother as he asked questions which he hoped were pointed and intelligent, covertly watching Melanie while Ethan responded, only half listening as he observed the girl's graceful movements from cupboard to drainboard. Once their eyes met and they smiled at each other in surprise and pleasure. After that Kip gave his full attention to his brother, certainly not wanting to appear gauche in his fascination with Melanie.

". . . fact is, most of our age group is tolerant of the worst slobs," Ethan was saying. "We get on the band wagon about an end to gun powder, but no one dances on the podium for old ladies who get their purses snatched every half hour. Why don't they start making a lot of noise about rapists and arsonists and the porno scene. . . ?"

"Wow!" Kip exclaimed, "you sound like a reformer. Dow would approve of that! Start talking like that around him, and he'll probably make out a check to your college sociology department."

"Well, if that won't do it, we'll let Melanie expound on the evils of Women's Lib."

Melanie giggled. "When the world gets to the place where grown men have to crawl into mama's apron, let me out. . . ."

"That from the future governor," Kip teased.

"When they get as liberated as Urliss, even, it scares me," Ethan groaned as Urliss retreated to the pantry. When the last dish had been dried and put away they moved in by the fireplace where they gazed wisely at the burning logs and thoughtfully at one another. "Christmas Eve. . ." Kip sighed. "This was the biggest time of the year when we were little, remember?"

"You sound like a jaded old man," grinned Ethan. "But I guess there have been a lot of changes, not all of them for the better."

Kip smiled shyly. "You have Melanie, that's the best of the better."

Ethan agreed. "You can say that again, but I'm plumb cynical about the state of the world in general, and why not? Look how we sit around, while the ocean turns into Mrs. Mulligan's diaper wash."

"You'll make a poor lawyer if you don't believe in progress," Melanie warned. "You do, don't you, Ethan? You believe there's hope for the world?"

Gently he reached out to cradle her face between his hands. "I believe that as long as there're folks like you and me and Kip, there's hope for the world."

"Now you're flattering us."

"I'm flattering the world."

Urliss poked her head through the door to suggest some games and withdrew from their intimate circle in annoyance. She was regretting not having asked John or Dow to spend the evening with them before they had been invited elsewhere. Never had she felt more alienated from Kip; not even those first few moments after she had met him were like this. Since coming to America she had never felt so alone. Christmas Eve was a time for family and loved ones to rejoice together, and she was being tucked away like an old keepsake in someone's wretched attic. For the tenth time she rinsed her hands, dried them on her apron, and peered through the window at the hearts and lights hanging in the back entry. Once more she went back into the big room.

This time the boys took their cue and turned on the stereo to play the old carols. With mock courtesy they led Urliss to a big chair near the tree and Kip started handing out the presents.

Half the Lutheran congregation had remembered Urliss, it seemed, their presents coming in so fast that Kip had stacked them neatly in two tiers that reached almost to the middle of the big fir. Urliss opened each article carefully and silently: aprons, bedroom slippers, mittens, perfume, a brush and comb set, even a hand-carved cross for the wall of her bedroom. Soon her composure began to crumble and tears slid down her flushed cheeks. Twice she had to leave the room in order to cry into a towel in the bathroom, returning each time with red, swollen eyes. Her fingers trembled as she opened more gifts. From her brothers in Norway she received a frilly bathrobe that spoke fluently of their hopes for her romantic opportunities to wear it. From her uncle she received a hand-knitted ski sweater. A long time later, after Kip and Ethan and Melanie had finished unwrapping their own presents and were waiting with polite little smiles, she ripped the flap off a plain white envelope which read: "To the Mermaid of the Midnight Sun for services beyond the call of duty, from Kip and Ethan." Inside was a reservation for one week at a ski lodge in the mountains.

Urliss stared at the slip of paper while she fingered, examined, marvelled. As the full impact of this generous gift swept over her, she retreated hastily once more to the bathroom, vowing into the towel never to leave those dear boys, "No," she murmured, "I vill stay forever in dis grim vilderness and cook for dem and dere children to come," ending up an old maid—the wind, blowing dust and tumbleweeds over her tombstone—Urliss Peterson, faithful friend, devoted servant. . . . The nostalgia and sorrow of her new martyrdom carried her all the way back into the living room where she sat meekly in her chair, too numb from emotional exhaustion to move.

But she was very tired and when she heard John's rig drive into the yard, she went to her room wearing her new slippers and cradling as many of her gifts as she could handle. With deep, pleasurable sighs she fell into bed.

The brothers and Melanie talked on into the night until only a ghost of a fire remained and the house snapped and cracked in the cold.

But they were up the next morning to take the jeep out and ski the coulees while a bright sun spliced the brittle air. Their skis splayed skillfully through the snow, but the fatiguing work of climbing the slopes after each maneuver heated them up so that soon they were shedding jackets and scarves. Finally, they piled wearily into the jeep and took the long road home.

"Melanie hasn't seen our town yet," Ethan reminded Kip. "Let's take the road to Ordlow."

"It's so big, this country," Melanie exclaimed excitedly as they went on. "To think of having a whole world to yourself! It isn't fair when most of us are crammed into cubbyholes."

"It surprises me that you like it," Kip exulted impulsively. "Doesn't it surprise you, Ethan?"

"This gal is full of surprises," Ethan said in a low voice close to Melanie's ear.

"I mean, she's so—so sophisticated," Kip hastily explained, feeling more like a jackass each passing second, "don't you think, Ethan—so citified?"

"City manners and a country heart," Ethan teased.

Kip's hands were clammy on the steering wheel. He felt awkward and self-conscious. They were coming close to the commune now and he slowed the jeep deliberately. "Wonder how they're faring," he muttered.

"Would you believe rheumatiz and starvation?" Ethan guessed. "What the good people of Ordlow County were helpless to do the prairie winter should take care of; come spring they'll all be gone. Or dead."

"They're not a bad sort," Kip said defensively; "pretty decent, actually. Several of them have gone to work around here as unpaid servants. The women put in regular shifts of volunteer work at the hospital."

"Crazy," Ethan said. At the corner of the gate leading to the driveway squatted a fat snowman holding a sign which read: "Jesus Is the Only Way to Life." "*That's* what I mean," he exploded; "anyone who'd claim there's just one way to live is about as smart as a cowchip."

"They act like they're convinced, anyhow," Kip said. "They take in anybody who needs help and share what they have." The strange blend of meekness and power exuded by the fanatics stirred some fleeting hunger in him so that he felt apologetic, even protective, about them.

"No doubt acting under the premise that the quicker they share their food, the quicker they'll starve and go to heaven."

Kip tromped on the floor board so that soon they were rattling across the railroad tracks at the edge of town. "Here we are, folks," he mimicked the tone of a sight-seeing guide, "entering the great little town of Ordlow, the little burg with the big, big heart. You'll notice Main Street is as wide as the Mississippi River. That's because they usta drive trail herds right down the middle. This here is a good, solid little town with lots of popular merchants." He steered up one side street and then another until they had covered the business section, and then pursued the west-side area, crawling slowly past Coach MacDougal's house with its pink shutters and matching flower pots. Ethan gave Melanie a wild, brief account of Kip's ill-fated football game where Urliss had tangled with the coach. Melanie gasped her astonishment.

"It's all resolved now," Kip hastened to explain. "MacDougal and his wife took Urliss to lunch and now they're friends."

Ethan guffawed. "Urliss buried her hatchet?"

"She says now that anyone can make a mistake."

"Meaning MacDougal."

"Naturally."

They all laughed.

When they reached the house Urliss was starting to set the table for dinner and Melanie took over, apologizing for being so late. "But I wouldn't have missed it all for anything!" she exclaimed through the residue of her baptism in prairie legend. "I'm trying to get everything about this country settled into my head. It has a style I'm wild about!"

Urliss bent over the oven and basted the turkey, her face expressionless.

"You like it here, don't you, Urliss? You're happy, aren't you?"

She shrugged. "Yah, I get used to it."

Carefully Melanie counted knives and forks and spoons and lined them up beside the plates. "It's the happiest Christmas ever!" she declared, still flushed with pleasure.

After the bounty of her table had made satisfied gluttons out of the brothers and she had raised her brows only slightly at Melanie who nibbled at her fruit soup and turkey, Urliss climbed up to her room to flop on the bed, warming her body under the big down comforter. She reminded herself of her part in making good Christmas memories for "de poor orphans" who had been happier than she had seen them at any time.

In late afternoon the brothers and Melanie climbed the windmill, all three of them squeezing onto the platform from which they could watch the prairie flowing away everywhere to a sky growing increasingly grim and unfriendly. Then they hitched the old Morgan, Pan, to the sleigh and rode through the eastern grassland until their faces were stiff with cold, caroling and laughing while the bells on Pan's harness tinkled softly. When darkness settled in like a black cape, Kip reined up and stared into the night. Not a star to be seen, not a single, solitary star.

"The stars are gone," Melanie said.

Kip nodded. "Smells like snow." He turned homeward where the yard light revealed hard, bitter flakes dancing through the air. Then the storm set in. The wind-hurtled snow stung their eyes and pommeled the old Morgan who patiently longed for his stall in the stable.

"What a way to live!" Melanie cried, "I think I'll come back here, Ethan, and spend the rest of my life riding the sleigh and curling up in front of the fire and watching the prairie move from dawn to dark, from quiet to storm. Oh, it is beautiful!"

Kip felt a lump rising in his throat as he listened, and then a hard, heavy hurting started in his chest, a hurting that spread all over his insides. He could not explain its origin, but he knew it had everything to do with his love for his brother and his undefined feeling for Melanie.

The holidays exploded into rockets of joy. On the last day of vacation Kip came down with the flu, a bug that made his limbs ache under their covers. He urged Ethan to leave as he had planned, but Melanie would not hear of it. "Nothing could move us today!" she declared and proceeded, without subtlety, to rob Urliss of the privilege of nursing him, making pitchers of hot lemonade for him to sip at and bringing him aspirin and cold packs for his head. When he awakened from cat naps she was seated beside him, her hands cool on his forehead. "Poor Kipper, Melanie will take care of you." Each time he protested about her exposure to his bug, she would smile patiently and continue to care for him. He felt both humbled and annoyed by her sacrifice.

While Melanie fluttered over Kip, Ethan set idly by, dividing his time between reading a book and watching them both with a mixture of pride and amusement, delighted that Kip and Melanie hit it off so smoothly. Once, when Melanie left the room, Ethan asked, "How do you feel about getting a sister, Kip?"

Kip smiled crookedly and shut his eyes, and then he opened them wide and examined his brother closely. "As fast as you go through girls, I won't get my hopes up," he said lightly.

Ethan laughed. "Fat chance I'd let go of Melanie."

"You're sure you'll always care for her the way you do now?" Kip prodded hoarsely. "I mean—uh, you're serious enough to—to *marry* her?"

"You bet. I've never been so positive about anything. She's everything I could want—more, even." He leaned back, cradling his hands behind his head.

"She shouldn't have stayed," Kip said, suddenly irritated. "You shouldn't have let her."

Ethan grinned. "I couldn't drag her away. She likes you, Kip—really likes you; she likes everybody. She's so great I'm a little awed by her."

The next morning, when he came out of a heavy sleep, Ethan and Melanie were gone and Kip's mood was as gloomy as the frozen, milky sky hanging low outside his window. "Melanie." Her name rolled over his tongue in silent wonder, her chirruping voice, her bubbling laughter echoed in every corner of the house. *Poor Kipper, Melanie will care for you. . . .* Again and again he felt the electric touch of her small hand. The intensity of his feeling for her now came with such overwhelming power that it seemed some force outside of himself had moved in on him.

He groaned with agony and remorse. She was Ethan's girl. He loved his brother more than his own life, and now he wanted his girl! Time and again he willed himself to turn his mind from imaginings that made him captive to emotions which both tormented and thrilled him.

But as the thought of Melanie flashed unbidden into his mind, the wonder of her attractions wove a web of paralysis over his conscience. He grew transfixed with visualizing how it would feel to hold her close and love her.

As the weeks passed she became an obsession. He thought of her almost constantly and, however laced with pain, it became the only pleasure he could claim. The rest of the time he was anxious and miserable, frustration giving in to quick anger and a defensive spirit. At school his grades slumped, he grew absent-minded and withdrawn, seeking no one's company. Even Urliss irritated him, and he thought he might be losing his mind.

But he would not give up the longing that made its fire-bed deep inside of him. He tried to console his conscience from time to time with the thought that it was no fault of his that he had crashed over his brother's girl.

8

The Proposal

I don't mind going out
to the wind—dark wet;
but not alone, not yet, not yet;
first someone to hold me near,
to walk beside me, someone dear. . . .

IT WAS THE TIREDNESS that got to Dow Garstin. Like an avowed enemy it dogged him, settling on his shoulders, slipping down his chest and into his legs until he felt boneless. He couldn't walk a mile without panting and even now, with Fontane single-footing beneath him and a biting breeze fanning his face, the tiredness nagged at him. Something in his body chemistry was off kilter.

The stallion's hooves crackled thin-crusted snow like dry willows breaking as he circled the feed-trough where cattle chewed hungrily at dusty hay. Dow reined up and eyed them patiently. Soon it would be calving time, another spring about to break.

As he turned home the thought of tea was comforting, too comforting. "Yeah, Fontane," he muttered, "the old man is molderin', soft and molderin.' "

But he was not old; he was fifty-four and had always been as strong as a bull. Suddenly, leaden with a bleak sense of having missed something, it came to him—with some surprise—that he had failed to experience the best part of life by never having had children. Unlike Ed Kettrie who lived on in his boys, Dow's life would end at the grave and strangers would occupy his fine ranch one day, neither remembering nor caring that he had built it from the timber of his own soul.

The thought had pestered him before, but he had measured it against his marriage which had ended with a Dear John letter while he was in a foxhole in Africa and against the merits of a bachelorhood imposed upon him by Ila Kettrie's inaccessibility. But now he let the full impact of his solitary existence sweep over him like a dirge. He tipped back his hat and squinted at the glare of sun on snow and encouraged bold scheming to override the usual caution of his nature with an urgency that demanded his complete attention. Weighing his need against the prospect of action as one weighs a strain of music, not only for its quality but for its fleeting impression which can neither be lassoed nor crystalized, Dow finally came to a decision. Tomorrow he would do two things: keep his appointment with Dr. Saxon and decide which available woman he would make his wife.

The first chore took most of the day. Dr. Saxon put him through all the paces of his clinic, pricking and probing and laying him out like a calf on a stake for pictures of his joints and prisms. In fact, he urged Dow to spend the night in the hospital so he could do some further exploring, a suggestion which made the baron laugh as he walked out of the office.

The next chore might take a bit longer. Last night, as he had spent hours making mental appraisal of the single women in the area, dismissing each one for a variety of faults, the Norwegian woman had come to his thoughts time and again; but he doubted that she would defer her headstrong lament for city grandeur to an ongoing life at the ranch. However, her attributes ruled out any obvious handicaps—she was loyal, responsible and capable and would make a fine mother for his sons; and if there was still doubt crawling around his head like a busy beetle in a haypile, the fact that she was the handsomest woman he had ever known cinched his decision to call on her.

All the way to Shellydown he thought about how it would be to have a son this late in years; there was so much he would want to teach him, and there might not be enough time to teach him anything at all. In the event he did not live to see his son grown, it was important he have a proper mother to complete the job, a woman of good breeding and character.

When he drove into the Kettrie yard, he spied Urliss through the window, her head bowed over some knitting; and then, when the dogs barked, he saw her get up and move away. He checked his appearance in the visor mirror. His good looks hardly betrayed the weariness crouching under his rawhide coat.

When Urliss opened the door she made smoothing passes at her hair. "Ah, Mr. Garstin, you look for John?"

"No," he smiled, "I saw John in town. It's you I'd like to talk with."

She seemed surprised as she backed up and opened the door widely. Swiftly Dow scanned the room. It was clean, comfortable, and cheerful, and his hostess who had drawn her hair to a braided coil on top of her head, her face devoid of make-up, was attractive and healthy. "Sit down," she urged, scooping up her knitting and plunking it into her sewing basket. A minute later she plucked it out again and re-wound it with quick, nervous hands.

Feeling stiff and unnatural, Dow sank into the wingback and perched his hat on his knee. Making small talk came hard for him, but he worked cautiously into his proposal. "Tell me if you've adjusted to this way of life," he said, examining her closely.

She shrugged. "I like dis house—and Kipper. I like Kipper most of all," she said, pronouncing her English carefully.

Dow was pleased. "Good, good. You like young people, children."

"Of course. If dey be good I like dem lots."

"Ever thought of settling down with someone, getting married, having a family of your own?"

The question was proper enough, but Urliss flushed. "Someday," she replied in a voice impassioned, "ven I have a man. . . ."

Dow continued to study the promising stretch of her.

"Vy you look so?" It was clear that she was finding his visit unsettling.

He cleared his throat, stood to his feet and began pacing up and down the room. "Do you think you could learn to care about me? Enough to live with me?" He stopped to look at her.

She had turned very white. Her hands shook so that she caught them together in her lap. "Vy you ask?" she whispered.

"Because I want to marry you." He was surprised by his own tongue. He had not planned to be so blunt, but he could not simply sit around talking about the weather.

She stared at her fingers which she splayed helplessly. "Ah, ve don't know each oder," she murmured thickly, "must courtship first, see how ve like each oder. . . ."

"There isn't time," he said brusquely. "Listen, I'm almost fifty-five. *Fifty-five*," he repeated. "I should've taken a wife long ago, but like a great fool. . . ." He stopped pacing and turned to her. "I've no time to waste, you see that. Naturally I want children, a son to inherit my holdings, that's most important. I'll probably live to see him reared, but in case I wouldn't, I'd want you to teach him to go in the right way." Catching the horror and disbelief in Urliss's expression, he shook his head and added, "I haven't handled this well. I've upset you."

She could not meet his eyes.

"Look at me, Urliss," his voice almost gentle.

But she had turned her head away.

"Think about what I've said," he persisted. "I'm serious about wanting to marry you. Tomorrow I want to take you to dinner. I'll come by at six. All right? We'll get acquainted."

She bit her lip and nodded woodenly. He walked over and took her hand very gently. "Don't be afraid," he said, smiling into her eyes, which she had raised for one imploring moment.

After he had left, Urliss broke into tears and ran to her room where she threw herself onto the bed and sobbed wildly into her pillow. It was not enough that Dow Garstin frightened and unnerved her; he had dealt the crowning insult by offering marriage to her as if he were purchasing a brood cow at an auction. She wailed brokenly, trying to work up feelings of outrage to cover her humiliation.

At last she dried her eyes and lay staring at the ceiling. "I do care for him," she admitted finally. "Someting about him stirs me, alvays did, even if I hate him for vat he did today—de beast. Even if I vill never marry him. . . ."

But her pen was already moving luminously through the dreaming orbit of her mind. *Dear Father and Brothers. . . Yes, I am to be joined in holy matrimony; the man is very rich and important, the owner of much land—a cattle baron. It will be a great wedding with hundreds of guests, and my gown will have a train as long as the aisle. . . .*

Finally she dried her eyes and blew her nose and thought about what she would wear tomorrow night, surveying her wardrobe through swollen eyes and deciding on a long beige skirt with a mauve lace blouse. Then she started to tremble with the shock and strain of it all. "Imagine it, oh, imagine!" She laughed and shivered as she thought of the foolishness and wonder of their coming together, of how it would be when he embraced her and whether she would faint dead away.

When Dow picked her up the next evening a grave, almost dolorous dignity encompassed her. But inside the large car her dignity crumbled when Dow told her that he would drive her past his ranch buildings, reminding her that this was the life-style to which his wife would be assigned. Outside, a bleak wind tore savagely through the coulees, muffling the lonely sound of cows bawling on the hilltops. Little spits of rain fell from a nervous sky that changed from streaks of light to dark and back again so that a depression fell over her spirits. Urliss looked at Dow for reassurance, wanting to say something bright and clever to ease her tension. Turning in the seat, she found herself staring into his deep, gray eyes. She gasped and quickly dropped her gaze, drawing on her gloves.

Husband. It was the first time that she had allowed the unbidden words free rein. *My husband.* She swallowed an urge to laugh. She must be out of her mind to be attracted to such a mad man. They were both insane to be thinking of sealing themselves to each other forever. If a child came from such a union it would be a strange, if not abnormal, creature. She grew stiff and silent again with the thought of it.

They drove past a large dam with visible patches of ice where the wind had swept away the snow. Beyond it lay a vast corral and rambling barn. She had heard that Dow Garstin was a slave for work. So he drives himself, she thought; he is not at rest in his soul, so he works, works, works. Ah, the poor beast.

Just as he said, "There now, here we are," she looked ahead at the vague outlines of several cottages and an attractive house with gables. A faint surprise increased her interest; she had not expected the house to be so big. Relief and curiosity lifted her spirits. "Who live in de small houses?" she asked, watching smoke curl from the chimneys.

"The cook, housekeeper, the hired hands. Well, what would you like to see?"

Although she was dying to see his home, she teased, "De barn vill tell me vat kind of housekeeper you be," peeping at him hopefully.

"The barn it is!" His eyes twinkled with fun and the sight made Urliss laugh aloud. She was still smiling when he stopped the Lincoln and opened the door for her. "You're not exactly dressed for such an excursion."

"Again, depends on your housekeeping," her voice lilted.

The barn was a vast dome with wings on either side, smelling of sweet hay and the warm breath of animals. From his stall a chestnut stallion whinnied lightly and Dow spoke to him softly as he guided Urliss to an elevated dais and lifted her bodily up over the ledge. The physical contact caused Urliss to flush with quick and powerful feelings. "See here," he said as he released her, "see what we have here."

In the corner beside the mother lay a cluster of new kittens.

"Oh, aren't dey sveet!" Urliss exclaimed dutifully—as if she were not plagued by the stray toms and laboring felines that filled the clefts of the hay mounds at Shellydown. "Ah, de little tiger, he's de choice vun!" she exclaimed in spite of herself, picking him up and stroking him, observing the pensive flickers passing over Dow's face. How fine that he should take interest in little new creatures, she thought. He has dimensions that are pleasant and endearing after all. She had misjudged him. Enigmatic he was, but deep and exciting also, even charming.

Next he introduced her to Fontane who tossed his black head jealously, his eyes wild and threatening as Urliss snatched back the hand she had extended to pet his nose. "I be afraid of him," she admitted.

"He's mine, this one." He rubbed the stallion's head for a moment and then turned abruptly away. "Time enough to see the rest later, better in daylight. Let's go." He guided her back to the car.

Inside the rambling, pretentious country club, Urliss did not miss the deference with which Dow was greeted. The head-waiter called him 'Senator,' and after they had ordered their dinners Urliss asked, "Are you political?"

"Everyone is," Dow observed, "to one degree or another. I served this county at the state level a couple turns."

"Ah," Urliss sighed, "a very important man you are."

Dow leaned toward her. "I will tell you something of myself." His eyes bore into her intently. "I pride myself on being a man of honor and integrity. With me honor is the staff of life. Remove it, and civilization breaks down and good men labor in chains. I hate cowards, traitors, and rabble-rousers, in that order.

"I'm an early riser. I don't eat breakfast for at least two hours after getting up. I like my main meal at noon. I had six years of college, part of it after the war. As a matter of fact, I taught history for a year at the university."

Carefully Urliss weighed all that he told her. "A man who plan his life vell," she said finally, smiling. "Excell—ent man," she added, her smile deepening, revealing her fine, even teeth. "I like order, also. But de order of my life has been—stuffy. I, too, like discipline, morals. I am Luteran," she added, nodding slightly, as if this explained the reason for all her fine attributes. She leaned forward, holding her coffee cup carefully with her little finger extended daintily. "Is important to me my husband should believe in God."

"Only a fool wouldn't," Dow assented. "I just hope I don't have to play second fiddle to Him." He smiled back at her.

Urliss relaxed pleasurably. "Is good." She laughed. "Is wery—wery good," she added carefully.

Dow ate his food with relish. Urliss was fascinated by the amount of food he consumed. For her part she picked gingerly at her prawns, nervous about chewing in his presence, even though a heady pleasure was making her as settled as an old tub. "Yah, I have nodding against money eider. I like to spend; be fore-varned." She watched carefully his reaction to her little joke.

"Thanks for telling me," Dow said congenially. "I'll make sure the checking account stays in my name until I've taught you the importance of austerity." His friendly smile belied the strength of his words. "I intend to be the head of our family. I will be good to you, but if you ever turn that famous temper on me, I will tie you to the bedpost."

Although his tone was relaxed, Urliss detected inflections of dominance. Her eyes flashed as she raised her chin proudly. "If ever you lay hand to me, you vill be befuddled of honor. And someting else. I vill be head of *house*. You can be head of barn and"—she gestured wildly—"vilderness. Da house hearkens to me!" Although her heart was in her shoes, she met his eyes boldly.

Dow measured her carefully. "I don't mind a little spirit," he said, "but only a little. I cannot stand a shrew."

She blinked. "Nor I," she agreed. "I cannot stand shrew or monster, neider vun!"

Dow cleaned up his plate and picked up the check. "Let's go," he said curtly. Stiffly he helped her with her coat and led her to the foyer. This is what I get for being an old fool, he thought as they got into the car and headed home. She is a stubborn, head-strong mare and too set to change. I need a gentle woman. Ila Kettrie's sweet face came to his mind, and he knew a yearning so forceful he groaned aloud.

In her corner of the seat Urliss was writing another letter: *Dear Father and Brothers, I am not to be married after all. The rich man who wanted me is a tyrant, and good I found out before it is too late.*

But her heart was pumping like a lead drum. The idea of los-ing what she had so hardly gained filled her with regret. When they reached the Shellydown cattle guard, she spoke in a small but firm voice. "I vould make good vife, it is true. But I vould have to be cared about vid respect.

Dow looked surprised. He mulled over her words. "I respect you very much, you must know that," he said with feeling. At her door he kissed her, steeling himself against the hungers surging through him like swift streams falling, plunging headlong into the charm of infatuation. He arranged to marry her in exactly two months.

Throughout the following week they were nearly inseparable, crowding into those days the courtship of their lives, caressing each other with admiring glances and restrained, tender hands, revealing themselves with long talks.

And one day he took her to his ranch house, feting her with his own prime beef and wild rice with swiss cheese after a tour of the big rooms that were spartan in clean, solid looks and masculine with great leather chairs and metal lamps. A handsome home, Urliss thought, reckoning how she would soften it with touches of chintz here and there without disturbing its character. "Vill do," she remarked later with satisfaction. "Is fine home for Urliss and Dow." And after that her spare time was given to the mental task of dressing it up to satisfy her own flair for warmth and color.

Dow found himself unlocking a brimming closet of opinions and grievances which he aired now with verve. He spoke proudly of the men and women of the sod, a rare and special breed. Ranchers were expansive and generous, like their mother prairie, but they were too noble to conform to herd disciplines. In fact, it seemed as if they were always in mortal combat with the bloated bureaucratic government and encroaching unions bent on organizing them all from the cradle to the grave, demanding their very souls in exchange for tilling the earth and riding leather. "They chip away at our freedom, making our prisons out of words like parity and soil banks. But we'll go out like a bright candle sputtering in the air made rank by the stinking coal mining and sniveling bandits of urbania."

But although he championed his rancher neighbors, he often denounced their jealousies and petty feudings and had only the rarest personal dealings with any of them. He was the giant among them—remote, high-minded and inscrutable—worthy of their respect.

In fact, he did not really know the farmers and ranchers at all and could hardly be classified as a typical native. He was a lonely figure, as uncompromising as his roots, his affinity for the prairie farmers finding expression only because they were products of the land and life-style that gave foundation and meaning to the nation.

Urliss weighed everything he said with grave consideration. She struggled to see the land through his eyes and discovered that the ranch had long been his mistress, that here in the vast plains he could defend all that he knew to be simple and good. He knew instinctively that one day the world would return to simplicity and the people would turn again to the land.

"Like de hippies," Urliss murmured.

Dow groaned, "Those carpetbaggers!" His frustration surfaced quickly.

"John say dey are de only honest vuns in dis country."

Dow glared fiercely. "You know my opinion of John."

"Yah, vell, he is a good man."

"No fool is really good. The leeches are everywhere, destroying us all. Fools encourage them."

"So. I don't vant to qvarrel. But I tink some of de smart guys are biggest leeches of all. Nodding is so simple to declare."

With the zeal of a prophet mounting his bench, Dow turned on her. "The left-handed radicals wield the power in this country. It's because of them the nation's become a jungle, people locked into their houses like pets in a zoo. You can thank the leftists: writers, film producers, educators—all of them advocating the vulgar and obscene, glamorizing lies and laziness. Yes, you can thank them for the crash of our integrity. I'd like to meet some of those wolves in sheep's clothing; I'd give them a good trouncing." He grew further incensed just thinking about it. "Those fool hippies out there are a classic example of what I'm talking about—victims of sick thinking," he concluded, as he pulled on his overshoes. "The neurotics in this nation outnumber the practical heads four to one." He shuffled to his feet.

Wide-eyed and solemn, Urliss looked deeply at him. "Is a puzzle to me, you and your America," she said softly and slowly.

"The fault's mine for troubling you, never mind." At the door he cleared his throat and turned to catch her to his arms. "So here I am," he said gruffly, "trembling like a schoolboy. How I long for you, dream every hour of the moment when you'll belong to me."

She clung to him. "Soon now, no more good-bye for us. I vill be beside you alvays." But even as she stood clinging, her eyes were wet and a hollow sadness came to rest in the pit of her stomach. "Lord Gud, vat is it? Vat you say to Urliss?" she murmured against his chest. But there was no answer. She only wept and rained kisses on the neck of this one for whom she had waited half her lifetime.

Reluctantly Dow released her and shut the door behind him.

The following Monday when Dow came home for dinner, the phone was shrieking off its cradle. When he answered it, Dr. Saxon's nurse explained that she had been trying to get hold of him for days. Cheerfully she informed him that the doctor wanted to go over the returned lab tests with him.

Dow was irritated. "I'll talk to him now if he's still in, or call him tomorrow," he said.

"Doctor always goes over the tests personally with his patients, Mr. Garstin," she said kindly. "May I put you down for eleven tomorrow morning?"

Dow hung up the receiver and went outside. Above him swift purple tore the stars from heaven and the great sky closed in, cradling the earth for its gentle storm. Clean flakes of snow caressed his face. As always in the wet wind he found his ears straining for the sounds of night, its creatures burrowing and hiding, the land throbbing with rebirth.

His mind churned with the tumult of thoughts too harried for clarity. If he had to have surgery or some treatments, he would take care of it before the wedding. Excitedly he thought again of Urliss, of the joys ahead for them both. By George, he was a lucky man to have such a woman for his own. She was everything he could have wanted, everything.

When Dr. Saxon came into his office the next morning, Dow was watching the goldfish flit back and forth in the small aquarium. "Mornin', Dow," the doctor said heartily, shaking his hand. With a perfunctory air he pulled up his chair beside Dow and took off his glasses. "The biopsy showed malignancy, Dow; we need to do an exploratory at once."

Dow appeared lost in thought as he gazed out the window where a cottonwood limb was scratching the glass in a blustery breeze; a sparrow hunched into its feathers while it rode the sashaying bough.

"You know, of course," Saxon went on, "that we have a number of recourses even if we find that the cancer has progressed a way. We do a lot these days with chemotherapy and radium; the surgery itself may take care of it."

Dow said finally, "I should've been a naturalist, Dave, should've concerned myself with goldfish and sparrows and wine on the table." He laughed. "Come to think of it, my grasp hasn't been much wider than that."

"I'd be the last one to agree with that, Dow. There's not a better man in this country than you are. And you still have miles to go."

Dow sighed and continued to gaze out the window. A great sadness filled his heart. He found himself saying, "I can't see getting carved up and burned and losing my boyish curls just to gain a few more sickly seasons. We both know I'm on my way to the last count. I think I had some hint of it weeks ago, but I couldn't consciously define it." With deliberate composure he stood and held out his hand. "Thanks, Dave. I always said I'd go out on my feet when it was time. I want to keep my record for honesty."

"Now don't talk like a fool, Dow. There's no sense in assigning yourself to an early grave when we don't even know how far the cancer has traveled," Dr. Saxon argued.

Dow grinned wryly. "We have a pretty good idea, wouldn't you say?"

The doctor shook his head in resigned disapproval. As Dow let himself out the door, Dr. Saxon's eyes followed him sadly. "I'll be in touch, Dow," he declared. "Give it some more thought."

At home Dow poured himself a snifter of brandy and carried it to his office. It was a big room with a huge roll-top desk and a wall of books. At one end he had placed a daybed. Often he slept here, the dogs stretched out around the stove's belly.

He stood with bowed head, scowling at the embers in the fire. An impression that he had stood thus somewhere long ago, staring into live coals, watching his life's tide dwindling like so many rain drops approaching dry sand, gave him a sense of primeval kinship. Then, too, there must have been a housekeeper chattering like a magpie. He had long been accustomed to closing his ears to Mrs. Heath's verbiage, but today it required untold restraint to keep from shouting at her to leave him in peace.

". . . shutter on the north wing is loose. The wind rocked it all night. I could hear it clatter from the cottage. I was so weary this morning I could scarce raise the body. . . ."

"I have work to do," he said curtly.

After she had left, Dow poked around his office, handling familiar items, touching the painting over the mantle. Some of his best hours had been lived out right here. Often he had hunted the fowl that fed in his grain fields, bringing home grouse and pheasant and duck, simmering them over the grate in the stove, simmering them slowly for long hours so that the meat fell freely from the bones. Long ago John Johnson, that Cheyenne half-breed, had come and they had sat in front of the big window together and watched the fields flow away, smoking in silence, each remembering a world that was simpler and grander.

He sighed—remembering, savoring. In the end it was the simplest things that gave a man pleasure and meaning, he thought. But, time later to poke around the ashes. Now he must get his affairs in order. With the discipline curried from years of self-mastery, he sat at his desk and labored over his accounting books. Finally he made a call to his lawyer. In mid-afternoon he headed over to see Urliss.

He found her scrubbing the kitchen in an old pair of jeans. "You cannot come in," she protested, making scurrying attacks on the coil atop her head. "Ah, dat you should see me so vill make you run out on me!"

He flashed a smile that was forced and wistful. "Never mind, you are still a fine-looking woman. Come. I want to say a few things."

Under a self-conscious bloom she crossed the kitchen and he caught her to himself. As if affection were not an awkward display he held her, feeling the soft, generous warmth of her body, feeling the promise in her with such agonizing force that his mind staggered under the heaviest sorrow. Ever so slowly he released her and steered her to the living room where he pushed her gently into a chair.

After some preliminary comments on the approaching spring, he said, "Now let me talk a minute. I feel I made a mistake in pushing you into a quick marriage. You were right. We should have taken our time, planned a wedding for you, to someone your own age. I'm old enough to be your father."

Urliss had become very still. "Vat is it, Dow? Vat are you saying?"

Softly intent, he replied, "I'm going to throw you a hard curve. Last week I had some lab tests taken. The results weren't anything to shout about."

Urliss became as rigid as a coiled spring. She studied his face anxiously. "So? Vy not?"

"I have cancer; incurable."

Urliss's jaw went slack as she blinked her bewilderment. Her lips moved silently as she sought to register a shock that had not yet found acceptance in her emotions.

"In fact," Dow went on apologetically, "my staying power for this world is a matter of time."

"Ahh—" her features had congealed into knots and seams. She jumped to her feet and hurried to him, raining kisses on his chin, his jaw, his neck. "Ve marry tomorrow," she whispered, her voice breaking hoarsely. "Ah, darling, my darling. . . ."

Gently he released her arms and moved back. His sigh came from some deep-down place within that was tired before the battle had begun. "The marriage is off, Urliss."

"Ah, vat ails you, Dow? I vant you, to belong to you!"

"So you can nurse my sick body? I'm full of sores—"

"I love you, I love you. I vould nurse you forever! Oh, Dow, don't refuse me!"

"I can do without the dramatics!" he snapped as frustration and weariness overpowered his feelings.

"Only because I love you! I cannot stand dis, I cannot!" She began sobbing wildly.

"You'd despise me soon enough." He wanted to tell her that she must save herself for a real husband, that this was the final, noble thing he could do for her.

She continued to weep—helpless, raging cries.

He stamped outdoors and jumped into his pickup and drove out of the yard.

But often in the weeks after that, Urliss went to his house and sat in the big office chair while he rested. In time Dow accepted her presence and was grateful for it. Even as his strength waned, their affection for each other grew until their love became a legend in Ordlow County.

9

Upward Bound

Come down from that mountain
so I can see you,
drunk with dreams, high dreams;
If you can't come down, call,
Call down, I say, to cheer my way
till I can stand beside you. . . .

WHEN THE PHONE RANG Kip was in bed and glazed with
the first stage of restive sleep. He opened his eyes wide and
stared, listening intently until he remembered that he had not
heard Urliss come in from her nocturnal visit to the Garstin
ranch and there was no indication of movement or response from
John's room. With muddled deliberation he weighed the tempta-
tion to ignore the persistent jangling before hitting the floor and
pounding downstairs.

"Hey, how's everything going?" Ethan sounded gay and
lighthearted over the phone, and Kip tried to gather his own wits
to match his mood.

"Well, John and I just celebrated our fourth day of batching.
We made a washtub full of spaghetti."

"Good. Hope you get real domesticated so when I come home
you can take care of me."

Yeah, well, those hound dogs sure liked my spaghetti."

"Pliney and Albert, huh? Keep hitting it, you'll improve.
Melanie's on the extension. Say hello."

"Kipp—er? Hi!" Melanie chirped.

Kip felt the blood pounding in his veins. When he finally

found his voice, it sounded like a loose string on a banjo.

"If you knew how much we miss you!" Melanie exclaimed. "We wish we were with you right now!"

"Next year we'll all be together," Ethan said. "There's a real doll I want you to meet. She's a friend of Melanie's. So, you see, we're making plans already. Hey, how's Dow?"

Kip's mind darted wildly. So conscious was he of Melanie's soft breathing that he could not sort out his thoughts right away. "He still lazys around a lot," he said.

"Imagine that," Ethan mused. "Is there a name to his sickness?"

"If there is, he isn't telling. One thing, he says we can hold the ranch together if we manage things right, so he's been going over the books with me. Urliss is still helping his housekeeper."

"You have a cold?"

"No."

"Sounds like your head's stuffed up."

"I was asleep," Kip confessed stiffly.

"Sorry," Ethan said; "we'll let you go back to bed."

"I don't mind talkin'. Glad you called."

"Sure everything's all right?"

"Couldn't be better."

"Well, good-bye, li'l brother."

"Bye, Ki-i-p-per."

"Bye."

Kip returned to his bed in a daze. Was he imagining that he had detected undertones of longing in Melanie's voice? And her words—weren't they meant to convey a subtle possessiveness? *We wish we were with you right now.* . . . Was it possible she cared for him in the same way he loved her? "Melanie," he whispered, over and over.

When he woke once more it was early morning and his heart was heavy and morose. As far as he was concerned, there was no good reason for getting up. Beyond the fanciful sphere of his daydreams, life was dull and dismal. To worsen matters, John had recently turned into some sort of nagging preacher, as if he had suddenly realized that the whole household was bound for hell if he didn't do something about it. Instead of greeting Kip with his usual considerate warmth, several weeks ago he had started hurling scripture at him like some wall-eyed Elisha.

"Though I speak with the tongues of men and of angels and have not love, I am nothing!" he would roar at seven o'clock in the morning while Kip was fogging his way to the bathroom. Kip glared at him and felt like telling him to shove off. "What's wrong with John?" he had asked Urliss. "Is he losing his marbles?"

But Urliss was so distracted with Dow's illness that nothing else seemed to register. "He is vid dose hippies too much, you tink?" she had suggested vaguely.

"Maybe. His waltz with misfits is bound to rub off on him sooner or later. But I don't intend to be a target for that holy nonsense," he added sullenly.

Then yesterday morning John's crazy behavior had reached a climax when he had insisted on saying the breakfast prayer aloud. "Thank you for this food and the promise of this wonderful day. You've commanded us to love all men and that includes being content with what we have and never coveting that which belongs to another. Make us true to you in all our ways. For Jesus' sake. Amen."

It was at that moment that Kip's suspicions of John's mind-reading abilities had been confirmed. He had no doubt learned the art from those fanatics who were witches and devils, after all. "Listen, John," he said evenly through a set mouth. "Don't you or anybody else try to act as my conscience. Understand? I'm sick of your moldy scriptures!" He shoved his chair back and glowered at John's bewildered face. "Just keep outta my business."

That night also, Kip was troubled, and did not rest well. It seemed as if something with long, tenuous feelers was picking away at his sleep. A corner of him burrowed deeper into his protective slumber. This went on for several minutes until this morning he had wakened with a start. Uncurling himself like a pliant whip, he opened his eyes to the first slender blade of day. And then he remembered what it was that had roused him. He had heard a car drive up and had supposed it was Urliss, but he had never heard her come into the house.

He fought his way into jeans and slippers and took the outside stairway with dispirited steps. As he turned the corner he glimpsed a low-slung sports job just before its motor revved and commenced backing toward the gate. His first thought was that the occupants had been put off by the dark, uncompromising look of the house and decided to retreat rather than disturb them. He ran to hail the driver and was caught in the sudden glare of headlights. The car braked to a stop. When the door opened he froze in his tracks. "Melanie!" Her name fell from his lips like crackling paper.

"Kipper?" she said uncertainly. Her voice was shrill and unnatural. "I wanted to see your ranch again. I had a little free time and, just on impulse, I took off, drove all night to get here." She shivered.

While a regiment of uneasy thoughts scuttled through his head, Kip said, "You're cold, come into the house." He went ahead of her and opened the door. Inside he pushed the thermostat up to seventy and turned on a light, motioning for Melanie to sit down. "I'll make some coffee," he said.

"Not for me." She perched uneasily on the edge of the couch, clutching a heavy sweater that fell across her shoulders like a cape. Her eyes were saucers of misery.

"I—uh—was asleep and—uh—not fully awake yet." Kip sat down in a chair close by, hoping he did not appear as shaky as he felt. His mind and his emotions did not seem to be working together. On the one hand he was charged with a surge of passion; on the other hand, apprehension. "Everything okay? Ethan all right?"

She nodded.

"You have a fight or something?" he forced a slightly lopsided smile.

She looked startled. "Oh, no."

"He know you're here?"

She fished in her purse for a brush and started pulling it through her hair. "No, I just came on impulse, like I said."

Into an awkward silence, Kip asked, "You want some breakfast?"

She flashed a grateful look at him. "I'm not hungry, but thank you."

Kip watched the pendulum under the clock case swing to and fro. It was five minutes until five o'clock. "Everything's sorta stale around here with Urliss away so much," he remarked, wondering why, when there were so many ponderous things to be discussed, he could not think of any of them. He sighed and studied Melanie who was hunched into a little lump. Her inert posture found its echo in his own spirit, shrunken with anxiety, numbed with ghosted dreams. He leaned forward, his elbows boring into his knees. "Why did you *really* come?"

She continued to brush her hair. Finally she looked squarely at him and said, "Because I wanted to see you. You know that, don't you?"

He sucked in his breath. "I guess. Yeah, I guess I know it."

Plopping the brush back into her purse, her voice spiraled with tension. "It's crazy. When Ethan's not with me, it's you I think about most of the time."

With rigid calm Kip tried to let that sink in. He opened his hands helplessly and let them lie palms up in his lap. "A couple years back I had this crush on a girl. Real bad. I got over it, though. Can't figure now what I saw in her."

She bowed her head. "You're saying it's a passing crush." From beneath hooded eyes she gave him a searching look. "Don't you care, Kip?"

"What if I said I did? What if I said I care so much it's the most hell-awful thing imaginable."

"Oh, Kipp-e—er," Melanie whispered intensely.

"What if, Melanie? Do you think you'd break off with Ethan? And if you did, you think we could go our merry way and just forget him?"

"I don't know. I'm all mixed up. I care for Ethan, too."

"Well, then, I think what you're doing is pretty low down. Pretty low down." He stood up and started pacing the floor. She was some babe, he thought, wanting her and hating her at the same time. She wasn't worthy of Ethan. "Me and Ethan are brothers; had you thought of that? Do you know what a brother is? No, of course you don't. Well, listen while I tell you. A brother is your second heartbeat. He's your good legs when your own are tired. He's your alter ego. Anything that hurts him hurts you twice as much!" He sounded harsh and violent. He glared at her.

Tears stirred in her eyes and made little moist paths down her cheeks. Not a muscle in her face moved.

"Don't cry," he begged with sudden contrition.

But still the tears streamed.

Impulsively he went to her, sinking down beside her and taking her hands with his own. "Listen, Melanie, I didn't mean to hurt you. It's both our faults; we had no right. . . ." But somehow she got all tangled up in his arms and he felt himself falling into butterfly wells of delirium. The agony of the past months crystallized to impale him on stalagmites of joy and desire.

And then John walked into the room.

Kip broke from Melanie and stood up, his face gaping with confusion.

But already John had turned to shuffle quietly away in his stocking feet, apparently unaware that his intrusion had been noticed.

"I'm sorry," Melanie whispered. "He saw us, didn't he? Will he tell Ethan, you think?"

Kip could not look at her. A hollow sadness in the pit of his stomach made him feel as if he would never laugh again, not ever.

"Maybe he didn't recognize me?" Melanie persisted hopefully.

Kip grunted. "He has the eyes of an eagle and the memory of an elephant. Just as well he learned what a rotter I am. He's known it all along anyhow."

"Don't talk like that."

Still Kip could not bring himself to look at her. "There's not a heck of a lot more for us to talk about one way or another. If you're gonna stick with Ethan, that's fine. Just keep away from me—and anyone else you might get churned up about."

She pulled her sweater back over her shoulders, preparing to leave. "If you say so," she intoned without emotion.

"You should catch some sleep before you start back. The east room is empty."

She shrugged. "I couldn't sleep." She crossed the room, a little slip of a girl dipped in honey and rose petals and dried under a new sun on a misty morning. She opened the door and closed it softly behind her.

Watching her leave, Kip felt sick clear through. A sick skunk, that's what I am, he told himself. He heard the car motor cough and drone down the lane. He went to the high, tiny cupboard in the kitchen where his father had kept his wines and groped for the first bottle and swallowed half of it without pausing. Then he tottered upstairs and crawled back into bed.

The next day he avoided confronting John—an exercise in dodging that he would develop with proficiency in the following week. Now that his weakness (he preferred to call it that) had been physically exposed, he felt lower than ever. He found himself growing increasingly critical of John as he traced over his faults with dogged regularity until he had reached the amazing conclusion that John was himself a scoundrel, that the opinions of Asa Klinger and a dozen others had struck pay dirt in their estimation of his character as a champion of evil forces. He concentrated on all the annoying little habits John possessed, like blowing his nose so loudly that you could hear him in any corner of the house and picking his teeth at the kitchen table.

Woven into the weal of his growing aversion to John was Kip's fear that Melanie, in a surge of conscience, would tell Ethan about her visit to the ranch. If she did that he would kill himself or leave the country.

But in spite of all his fears and recriminations, he could not forget Melanie. Even those forbidden moments of holding her had intensified his obsession. In close running to his regular dream was a new sequence: the vision of Ethan tiring of Melanie and telling her to shove off. After which she and Kip would get together. This dream excited and pleased him and did not conjure up such guilt because it was a plausible happenstance.

On Saturday morning Kip was eating a breakfast of ham, eggs and biscuits when John came in from choring and set about fixing his own food. "That old red Beulah had a calf last night," he announced cheerily. "Tiny little mite he is, but he's on his feet and gettin' his dinner."

Kip gulped a glass of milk and started wolfing his food in order to get away.

"The calving will soon be coming on full," John reminded him jovially.

Kip said nothing.

While his ham sizzled in the frying pan, John sat down with a cup of coffee. "You got circles around your eyes and you're so skinny a good wind'd blow you away. You not feeling good?"

Kip forced himself to meet his eyes. "I feel fine," he said evenly.

John studied him for a minute. "No, you don't. There's somethin' ailin' you, eh? Maybe you need to let Doc Anderson look at your tongue."

Through gritted teeth Kip spoke. "Keep outta my affairs, John, you hear? Don't play father confessor with me!" Into John's bewildered face he tossed a sly insult. "I know now why you're always lending folks a hand, because you're a nebby busybody and other people's problems liven up your own stupid life." He grabbed his jacket and shot out of the house.

"Kip!" John called, racing after him. "Wait, son, wait!"

But Kip shoved the jeep into gear, careening explosively on ice in his haste to get away. All morning at school he nursed his hatred for John, staring through his science book as he read and reread a chapter with inverted vision, gliding to and from class like a Doberman sniffing its prey. He thought of additional insults he should have hurled at John and savored them for later.

After school he stopped at the Garstin ranch. When Urliss opened the door her face was closed, as if she had pulled a shutter over it. She lowered herself heavily into the big rocking chair and pushed it to and fro like a creaking metronome.

"Where's Dow?" Kip demanded, irritation mounting in his voice. This was some welcome.

"Sleeping," she replied, her tone indicating that he should know that Dow would be asleep at 4 o'clock in the afternoon.

A happy place, Kip thought glumly. Aloud he said, "You're acting like an old lady, Urliss. Wonder what it would take to liven you up." He grinned without feeling the slightest bit of mirth.

As if she was tearing off a shroud, Urliss came back from wherever she had been. Now her face was slack with hurting. "You know dat he's going to die, don't you?" she said so softly that for a minute he wondered if she had really spoken at all. "Cancer. He has cancer."

Kip reacted dumbly, letting the message soak in. He could not speak. The news should not shock him too much. The world was full of death. He should be getting familiar with that dark angel. He sat down on the cobbler bench.

Strangely, instead of regret he felt a peculiar sense of guilt, as if he himself were responsible for Dow's sickness. He sighed and leaned his head back against the wall and stared at a scar in the dark beam overhead. It was a dirty, lousy world.

"In World Culture today we had a session on How to Choose Your Life's Goals?" he told Urliss, punctuating his sentence like a question. "Last week it was on How to Be Successful?" Although he was not sure he had her full attention, he saw that Urliss was looking at him. "I don't get it, do you? Can't you see, we spend our whole lives learning how to live and—'whammy'— we're out of it? It doesn't make much sense."

"I love him," Urliss said simply.

Kip was stunned. He saw in her eyes the awful pathos of her soul, as if it had given birth to a malformed child. Impulsively he crossed over and knelt beside her, putting his arms around her. "Urliss," he murmured, "I wish I could make you feel better." But right away it came to him that it was himself who needed comfort, needed a salve for the wound of his own spirit, for the unreasonable guilt gnawing at his soul like a determined rat.

"Did I ever tell you about my dad?" he asked, sitting back on his haunches. "When he laughed it was earsplitting and sort of like he was moving musically up a scale. Well, we have a key on the piano that would vibrate every time he got to whooping it up. My mom was proud of his ability to make that key ring!"

Urliss formed her lips into a crooked half-smile. "And your mother, Kip, she play de piano a lot?"

"Sometimes. She couldn't carry a tune in a barrel, though. She'd try singing sometimes, in a funny little voice—" He broke off, remembering something Aunt Molly had told him before she had died. Dow Garstin had been in love with his mother, Molly had said. Long ago he had asked her to marry him and when she had refused him for Kip's father, he had caught someone else on the rebound and their marriage had not lasted any time at all.

He went back to the bench and sat down. He felt like a great clod of sadness. He did not want to go home where John's reproachful eyes would hound him to apologies. With Urliss he was pulled into that heavy vacuous silence of twilight that comes like a shallow thief stealing the glory from the day.

Before long Dow got up from his bed and the evening hours were whiled away, at his insistence, in going over farm matters. He suggested that Kip sell all the calves the next fall instead of keeping the select steers for special graining, that he trade the oldest combine in on a new hay baler and have most of the grain custom cut. He suggested a five-year program for possible herd growth based on fluctuating stock prices and available pasture-land.

When Kip finally found his way to bed, he fell immediately into the escape of a deep sleep full of roving images and traumas. He dreamed that Ethan had a golden spaniel puppy which he prized highly and kept protectively in his own room. Unknown to him, Kip took the puppy out for a while every day and played with it. He did not mean to hurt the little cocker; he only wanted to pet it. But somehow the puppy's affection changed so that when Ethan called him he would run to Kip.

With choking whimpers Ethan ran away, through the fields and coulees, toward the Reservation. Kip ran after him, calling, "Ethan, come back, I love you. See, I've put the little dog back in your room. I won't take him out again."

But all he could hear was Ethan crying. "It's ruined now, ruined," he called through his tears as he became swallowed up by the prairie.

"Ethan, come back, come back. . ." Kip's cries turned to moans in his twisted bed sheet. He awoke in a sweat.

For a long time his eyes turned listlessly inward. A sense of self-loathing washed over him. He saw himself as a little dark spot on the backdrop of forever and amen.

Suddenly he bounded from bed and threw on his clothes. Shivering from emotional stress more than the crisp, cool preliminary dawn, he pulled on a warm coat and boots and trekked as quietly as possible downstairs and outside.

The barn light was a small yellow fuse in the spangled gloom; the outlines of the buildings and slopes were ghostly in air so brittle with cold that a creak in the corral sounded like a gunshot. As Kip plodded down the lane and out the gate, the snow crunched and squeaked under his boots. He followed the country road. The frost was already nipping at his toes and face, tender yet from the blizzard frostbite. And as his thoughts ran ahead on the road, he admitted that his conscience had made a wretch of him all because he had fallen head over heels for his brother's girl.

John's face came to mind, with its dark, craggy, good looks, and he felt sad, remembering how the half-breed had taught him to ride and rope and take his bumps like a young brave, serving as friend and teacher right alongside his father. It also came to him that the bitterness he felt against John was partly directed at John's God who must have had something to do with the bum rap assigned to Kip in the loss of his folks and his frustrated love-life.

"Who is God, anyhow? Is He my enemy? Yes, He's my enemy," Kip decided. The way he felt, God was out to get him. The thought brought a sense of dread and foreboding in its wake so that a series of shrill, yipping sounds converging on him made his heart fall away, trembling with sudden fear. And then his befuddled attention was drawn to a gray fox terrier barking sharply as it circled him widely, round and round.

"There now," Kip whispered, crouching down and putting out his hand. "Poor, ragged little orphan; where'd you come from?" Shivering and whining, dragging its head pitifully, the little dog drew closer, its fearful shudders gradually succumbing to the warm nest of Kip's arms. "Poor little orphan," Kip repeated, thinking that the dog was not too unlike himself, lost and cold and frightened, needing someone to love him and reassure him. He had a fleeting impression of the little spaniel of his dream.

A longing for his dad's firm touch swept over him, and he thought again of John. The humble and gentle power of this man set you to listening and straining for a hint of some mystery that Kip had always chalked up to the ghosts of John's Cheyenne ancestors doing their toe dance in the background. But he knew there was more to the half-breed than that; and suddenly he recognized beyond any doubt that John had God. If anybody ever had Him, John did. He turned around, still cradling the little dog, and walked intently back the way he had come.

At the house he poured a bowl of milk for his new friend and set him on the rug under the kitchen table. Then he went as quietly as he could up the stairs and when he reached John's door he tapped gently with his fingers. "Hey, John, you awake?" he whispered.

As quick and silent as a cat John opened the door wide, his kindly face flushed with sleep but already alert and ready for anything. "Come in, son, come in," he said in a husky voice.

Kip went in and dropped into the only comfortable chair. "John, are you *wide* awake?"

"I'd say so, yes," John grinned.

"I need your help, John. I got this monkey on my back, giving me fits, and I want rid of it. What do you say, can you help me?"

John's eyes were warm and shining. Peering intently at Kip he reached for his old, patched Bible and set it down beside him as he straddled a corner of his bed. "Only one way to handle it, Kip. You've come to the place where you're willing to seek help for what's bugging you. And there's only one person who can help you. That's Jesus.

"That monkey on your back is guilt, the guilt we all accumulate when we insist on doing things our own way. The Bible calls 'doing our own thing' sin. And the only way to get rid of sin and the guilt that hangs on us is to repent, to change our minds about who is going to be boss in our lives.

"Jesus died so that you could get this monkey off your back and start all over with a clean slate. He knows how to make something very beautiful out of your life, Kip."

Kip nodded slowly, not in the least surprised by John's quick understanding of his need and hoping that what John said was as true and good as it sounded. A sense of eager excitement welled up in his chest.

"Now listen here, son," John opened the Bible and started to read. "Jesus said this: 'If the Son sets you free, you will be free indeed.' And this: 'It was not to judge the world that God sent His Son, but that through Him the world *might be saved*.' Do you see, Kip, you can be free from fear and guilt and the power of sin that make you drift and fall? God opened the way to bring all us rebels to Him."*

"Why'd He do that, John? How could He lay it on His Son that way? Seems a good dad would take it on himself and spare

---

* John 8:36, John 3:17—The New English Bible.

his boy. And how come He made such a rotten world anyhow?"

"First, He made us and this world for His pleasure and also because He wants to share His joy, His very glory, with His creatures. It's in His fellowship that we find meaning and security. To the degree that we leave Him out of our spirits, to that degree we find the world a vale of despair. Where man is separated from God, that's where real suffering comes. It's because *we* want to be gods; you see that? It's because *we* want our own way, dark and selfish though it might be.

"As for laying it on His Son, Kip, the Father came and paid the price in Christ, the Man. The creator God humbled himself. He came as a servant to His rebel creatures and made himself vulnerable to the worst they could do to Him. That's why we say, 'God is love.' He wanted to bring us back to himself so we could share His glory!

"He suffered in order to bring us salvation from death, to bring us God-life. All we have to do is invite Him in to lodge in our spirits."

"That's all?"

John nodded. "It's what we call the new birth. It's the Holy Spirit of Christ getting a hold on you forever. You turn away from going your own way to going God's way. The center of your life is no longer 'self' but Christ."

"You mean God is inside me?"

"Yes, Kip, that's it. Once that spirit of yours receives Christ, it will grow through your prayers and obedience and feeding on the Word. And you'll become more and more like Him!"

"I see," Kip whispered slowly, his face reflecting the wonder of truth breaking across his mind and some inkling of the holiness and goodness of such a great God. A sense of shame and unworthiness pulled at his mouth and he struggled against crying like a baby right there in front of John. "Yeah, I'm ready, John."

"Give me your hand, son." When Kip clasped his big hand John prayed, "Now Lord, Kip here doesn't need any introduction from me to you; you've known him all along. But he wants to get to know you. He's going to invite you to come into his heart to be his constant companion. And I thank you, dear Christ, that you will save him from death and darkness and lift him into the light and joy of your holy presence. Thank you, Jesus, for being here. Amen." He waited a minute. "Now, it's your turn, Kip."

Kip moistened his lips, his eyes squeezed shut in concentration. For a little time he was silent. Finally he said, "Lord, you know I'm a mess and need help. Please forgive me for those things I've done wrong. I sure appreciate being died for and becoming your child." Suddenly he felt close to tears again, felt the last of his manhood drain away, to be replaced by this helpless baby. "Thanks a lot," he added.

Tears were making John's face glisten like pulled taffy. Kip had never seen him weep before. They hugged each other, sensing the special quality of this moment, a moment for remembering. "Take this Bible, son, and read the book of John first, and then we'll talk about it. You're on your honeymoon now; you need to be alone with Christ for a while. Ah, Kip, how I praise God for bringing you into the kingdom."

"I have the greatest respect for you, John, always did."

"You know this makes me your spiritual father; what a humbling experience." His voice shook with feeling.

"Say, I like that." Later, as Kip turned to leave, he added, "You were always a second dad to me, John." He went back to his room and attacked the book of John like a hungry man his dinner. But after a while he got so excited he jumped up and started pacing the length of his room. "Boy, I admire you, Christ. You came to a world of aliens and self-righteous religionists who dogged your heels with jealous criticisms everywhere you went. How alone you really were. You took on the whole world, and you showed us who God really is and what He's like!" As he spoke his appreciation for Christ, for the price He had paid for him, personally, the sufferings of the cross took on new meaning.

Kip's attention was suddenly drawn to the sun stealing through his window. It seemed as if everything inside and outdoors was suffused with luminous softness; everything was good and beautiful and full of light. "I'm full of light, too," he murmured, "full of light and peace and joy, all washed inside. It's almost more than I can take in." How quickly it had happened, how quickly he had changed. "Well, I'm yours, Christ. You paid the price for me, and I want to please you. Musta been like your children killing you," he thought, sorrow coming over him like a fresh wound breaking. "I love you," he whispered. "I really want to know you." Once more he looked around his sunny room, observing how every stick of furniture and even the tiny pattern in the wallpaper stood out sharply. I feel all clean and at rest inside, he thought. I'm honestly happy! He laughed out loud. "Thanks for the gift of your friendship, Jesus. John's right. You're the greatest trip there is."

So he had to tell Ethan! He threw open his bedroom door and took the stairs like a gazelle.

Ethan, I found a treasure. . . .

You're a dreamer, Kip.

Ethan, I've seen the light. . . .

Show me the lights of Main Street, man!

With trembling fingers he dialed Ethan's number. But he was not in the dorm and had left no message. Well, he would call him later; right now he would get back to the Book.

But no sooner had he started on the book of Mark than a sweet, deep sleep came to him, and he rested all that day and most of the night.

Over at the Community of Helpers, daylight was crawling in like little glowworms when Annabelle's squawks and moans wakened Anna Vladmore who jumped up and ran to the tormented girl and shook her out of her nightmare. Then she held her in her own long, thin arms, caressing her and crooning. It was only one more moment in the mending of a torn spirit. This type of work went on hourly, daily, as Christ used them all to heal the bruised, bleeding wounds in the minds of those like Annabelle Lee who had been used for the twisted lusts of an unspeakable creature named Cola and his swarm of animal friends. Better she had died, Anna Vladmore thought bitterly, her own helpless tears flowing in sympathy.

"There, dear, dear sister, Jesus is here. He has His big, strong arms around you." (Hear me, Lord, this girl needs some more of your healing love right now.) "There now, think about Him; just let your spirit reach out and touch Him. He'll dry your tears; nothing will ever hurt you again." Oh, Lord, she muttered under her breath and in between her cluckings.

Soon it was time for Annabelle to get up and go to work in the kitchen, but Anna offered to take her place so the poor girl could go back to sleep. "No," Annabelle refused, "I need to get up and get busy. I must, you see, I must."

So Anna made their beds and tidied up and brushed her hair and then, with a great sigh, kneeled for her prayers. But from down the way came the soft mewings of Betty's baby, so she grabbed her sweater and hurried outdoors where the new sun was already sparkling and dancing over the diamonds of frost, crisp and still in the bristling cold. "Ohh, I love your sky," she whispered at Him seated on His throned vigil far beyond the luminous blue overhead. "If I could sing, I would create a praise anthem about how beautiful you are, Father God. . . ." She hugged her sweatered arms, bending into the early chill as she stepped through the crusts of ice that had formed between the ruts of the car tracks in the yard. And then her heart started pumping excitedly, as if it knew something her head did not. Sure enough, in a minute Kip Kettrie's pickup broke into view, and her busy heart started fluttering the more as she stumbled into the shy urgency of trying to get back into the shelter of the lean-to.

But Kip had spied her and was already steering through the gate so that, as the vehicle came crawling right up beside her, she thought she would faint away from happiness and dread.

From the first time she had laid eyes on him, he had caught her fancy so that she often felt her insides weaken when she glimpsed his truck or jeep going by on the road. On those rare times when he had pulled into the yard, lumbering out of his rig in that lazy, long-limbed manner that had grown familiar, she would feel her heart shrinking away and would run and hide, peeking out from around the corner of the shed from time to time until he had left. Sometimes in her dreams she had dared to pretend that she was pure and untouched by the ravages of sin, and worthy of this gentle, beautiful young man who needed only to know that Jesus was God in order to be the most wonderful man who had ever lived.

"Hello, you're Anna, aren't you?" He smiled from the open window of his rig.

She smiled back, glad that he knew her name and that she had taken pains with her hair, brushing it all the way to her waist. "Anna Vladmore," she said softly.

"Well, Anna Vladmore, I've been born into God's family. What do you think of that?"

Her heart nearly stopped beating. Like other prayers that were answered quickly, it was too good to be real, and she thought she would do something ridiculous like screeching with joy. "Praise God," she whispered, staring at him intently, "oh, praise God." And then she did the dumbest thing of all. She started crying, her face getting all wet and contorted, until she covered it with her chapped hands. Kip was no comfort at all. He only sat and surveyed her calmly. "When you're through crying, I'd like to take you to breakfast in Ordlow," he suggested.

She nodded agreeably while peeping through her fingers at the path and went off to tell the brothers that she was going away for a while. And then she quickly dashed some drinking water on her face and dried her fingers and rushed out to jump into the seat beside Kip, letting her breath out very softly and slowly in a long expulsion of relief. Before long all the frowns and griefs of the world's sorrows went floating away in the contentment of this new and special fellowship. She listened as Kip told her about his brother and the passing on of his parents and how John had led him to Christ. But when he told her about Dow being doomed to die, she recalled how she had gone to the baron's home and had railed at him and how he had helped her when she was trying to rescue her calf and helped her again when the bullies had attacked her and Bobby. A terrible sorrow fell over her so that once more she wept, struggling to compose herself and vowing that she would intercede for Dow Garstin every day until his soul was saved from darkness. "I'll pray for him, Kip, and so will all the Helpers. Why, he might even be healed of his cancer. We saw it happen once. A poor soul was healed of cancer, and he didn't even know the Lord. We just kept praying for him and loving him to Jesus!"

Kip nodded soberly. "Anything seems possible to me right now," he said.

Anna was pleased. She felt free of her burdens, free as a swallow flying high on its wing in a summer morning; but too high to see anything below except soft, green fields, too high to observe the little vulnerable creatures burrowing and trembling. "What a lovely spirit you have," she said to Kip with sudden boldness.

"What a lovely witness you'll be for the Savior!"

They sipped hot coffee from heavy mugs, and Anna ate her crisp bacon, savoring the taste and treat of it along with the wonder of this time. She was overwhelmed by the wonder of a spirit newborn into the kingdom, as well as the wonder of her fellowship with this excellent boy. She wanted to toss back her head and laugh to express her joy.

Kip was looking at her intently, as if he was coaxing some confirmation from her. "I hope I never lose this happiness inside me," he said.

Anna hesitated. "You're enjoying the 'first-love' time with Christ, Kip; it's a very special time," she reminded him gently. "But this first ecstasy will probably pass, and you'll go on to trials and stumblings and ups and downs, all of which will bring you to a steady and intimate relationship with Him."

Kip seemed to think about that. "No stumblings for me, little girl. I want to get right down to business."

Anna laughed. "You are exceptional, Kip. I knew it from the first time I saw you—the night the barn burned, remember? I wouldn't be surprised if you found a shortcut to the holy life."

Kip grinned. "Now you're talkin' like a wise little lady, and just for that I might crowd you with questions in the days ahead."

"Brother Ben is much wiser in the Lord than I am," she said meekly.

"But not half so pretty and sweet," Kip teased.

She flushed, her heart throbbing and hammering with the little birds in her tummy flitting around.

When Kip brought her back to the Community of Helpers, she went racing to her spot in the lean-to where she flopped onto her bed, hugging the pillow to herself, recognizing in her rapture that she was crazy about Kip.

It wasn't very long, though, before Anna felt something deep inside her breaking all up into bits and pieces, and sadness quickly filled up that newly formed hollow as her past loomed before her, hateful and ugly. The ruin of her then was the bane of any meaningful relationship with a good man now. No, she could not have Kip even if he might want her. She was not good enough. Heaven knew it and would never encourage it; purity always found its own level when left to the dear Father. So with her loving heart she prayed, "Father, give him a wife that's worthy, a saint of a woman, a virgin and meek and gentle. And for me, dear Lord, if you will, a boy who's had a similar background to my own, but one who loves you now with all his heart."

She got up and brushed her hair. She was late for devotions with the brothers and sisters. She must go over to the schoolhouse at once.

10

The Long Farewell

Come, lost lover, walk with me
Just to the pad of the raging sea,
I promise then to slip softly away
to the dark wet wind moaning astray. . . .

SPRING OFTEN COMES to the prairie with a great burst of
chinook and sun, but this year the balmy days alternated with a
howling wind that was full of pollen and promise. The first flecks
of green pushed through the matted grasslands and the hilltops
heaved thin streams of melting snow to the winding creek that
roared and churned furiously as it spilled over the flooding
banks.

Everywhere rebirth kindled the long lanterns of hope. A new
year, the farmer rejoiced; it has the feel of a good year. And his
wife, looking ahead to harvest, murmured that Son starts college
next fall or Daughter needs a piano, as she fluttered around her
man with warm coat and thermos, feeling his haste and pride in
getting the seed into the ground, feeling his need so deeply that
she was brisk and angry and glad all at once.

The lean trees in the coulees were singing their dark anthems
when Dow Garstin climbed the ridge for the last time. In spite of
a chilly gale, his face and hands were moist and he felt weak from
the exertion of his hike. Once more he looked around at the far-
flung rolling pastures and the clouds sailing like low barges
across the sullen sky. He noticed a few stray cows in the west pasture pawing at the new green under the couch and creeping
jenny, but above all these was the terrible familiarity that
mourned with the strain of things changing and passing away,
going to their death without protest. And while he looked, his fin-

gers fondled the revolver in his coat pocket.

It was a proper day for dying with the new spring hiding her face behind a silver wind and a moldy sky pressed in close to the earth. To know that he would not go out by inches like a worm on a stake, that he would die a whole man, gave to Dow the satisfaction that he was yet master of his own fate.

He was not afraid to go—he had outlived his era and was already a stranger to the changing tides. But he knew a pervasive loneliness for the son he had never had, the great things he might have done. He might have added his own cry to the trumpeted warnings going out across the nation to the rushing masses. Their monotonous sea of look-alikes were all bowing to the same crude, formidable masters with their picture tube thrones beckoning individualism and genius to the cellar in order that the dull and lazy and immoral might share their bread equally. Once he had tried. It was right after the war and he had single-handedly organized the Patriots for the Preservation of the Constitution. Couched in nationalist principles, they had sought a complete overhaul of the judicial system. In spite of pushing himself beyond his strength, the order had dropped into the growing drum-fire of social causes like an ice cube in the campfire, and he had been powerless to breathe any political clout into it. Then after his stint at the state level, he had withdrawn from the political arena, regarding it more and more as a masquerade for security and self-aggrandizement. Ah, well, too soon he had surrendered, the fight gone out of him, the vision dimmed.

And then he tossed his regret away. He was a conceited fool to think anyone would listen to his stilted anachronisms. A people demanding band-aid panaceas for the ills of their society must regard his like as rabble-rousers, to be dismissed without curtsy. Yes, he had correctly understood his position among this generation. It made him angry to think of it. He could tell them all that the solitary crier in the streets is often the unsung hero of history. He it is who keeps us roused from reverie and fat complacency. He it is who calls us to examine, to weigh, to act with conscience and foresight. No pied piper, him, no masses weaving alongside to spew out their dark threats.

His anger was replaced by a hollow sadness, calling him to unshed tears. But he was not one to weep, no, never had since he was just a boy. Once more his hand curled lovingly around his silvery Smith and Wesson.

At Shellydown Kip was looking everywhere for a calf whose mother seemed to have birthed it still and lifeless or else abandoned it in a spirit of rejection, so swollen and heavy was her udder. Still, it was possible that the young cow had planted her newborn in a secret place, knowing that instinct would keep the little creature immobile until she returned from grazing or drinking or whatever mission she had assigned herself.

Kip drove his rig as far as he could through the fields and then tramped on foot into the swales beyond the meadow. Following the fence that separated Kettrie land from Garstin's, his eyes strained into the little pockets where a tiny calf could be tucked away. About to circle back he spied the little cinnamon creature stashed part way down a cove, above the mud, yet low enough to be protected from the wind. Kip laughed. The maternal jealousy of the mother cow made him feel warm and glad. He was filled with admiration for the Creator who had woven a pattern of protection and love into ever facet of life. Everything in his world had taken on holy meaning since his encounter with Christ, and his fellowship with Him these past months had grown so deep and precious that even John shook his head at how fast he was stabilizing and growing. "All in the world I want," Kip frequently told him, "is to let Christ live His life through me." Now, as he watched an eagle soar overhead, he thought about how God had changed his life. The Holy Spirit was purifying his thought-life and drawing his attention to the sins of subtle pride and self-centeredness that were holdovers from his old days.

At first he had been dismayed to learn that the power of the tempter was just as keen after his conversion; that, in fact, his capacity for sensual love seemed whetted to fiercer heights in the awakening of his spirit. He recalled the battles he had waged in his obsession with Melanie and how, finally, he had come to the end of himself and had given it to Christ. Only then had he realized his first complete victory over the power of his own imagination. He also had learned something about the power of mutual thought assent, because now that he no longer craved after Melanie, she appeared to have lost interest in him, also. Now they were free to build a new relationship based on respect for each other in their brother and sister kinship through Ethan.

His thoughts matching the flight of an eagle winging into the low sky, Kip noticed Dow silhouetted on the distant ridge. No doubt he was checking herds through his binoculars. This meant he was having a good day. He hesitated and then decided to go over and talk to him.

Step by step, Dow was teaching him the business sense of operating a ranch; but if Kip had learned to feel comfortable with him, he had yet to break the older man's reserve. "Halloooo!" Kip called, raising his arm in greeting when Dow turned his head ever so slightly. As he drew closer he saw that Garstin was standing very still, his coat flapping in the breeze, his shoulders hunched like a curved bow. Then he saw his face—gray and set hard. Kip attacked the ridge with giant strides.

Dow felt as if someone were cutting through his innards with the dull edge of a knife. His astonishment at the intensity of pain turned to grimace and for a moment he could not breathe. "Go away," his eyes glowered at Kip, but his vocal cords were impaled on stalagmites. As wave after wave of searing pain tore through him, he was dimly aware of the boy's stricken posture and of his voice raised to heaven. He was amazed at the agony a man could endure and still live. As the pain let up he felt sick and faint. He cursed himself for not having used his revolver three minutes sooner and cursed the bitter irony of Kip's trespassing. What the devil was the boy doing here? The whole affair, so carefully plotted, had turned into a comedy of errors, leaving him with the feeling of being set adrift on a churning sea in a small, oarless boat. . . .

The next morning Urliss stood in the doorway of the den, watching Dow Garstin while he slept. It seemed to her that his powerful spirit filled the whole house even when he was not awake. Every day now she had been with him, watching him as he sat in his great chair, warming himself by the stove that was full of the sound of wood snapping and air being sucked up into the chimney. There he often stared ahead of himself in silent introspection, dozing fitfully as the day wore on. Noting each flutter of his eyelid, a wrench of his mouth, a trembling nerve in his wrist, she had sat beside him, solicitous and composed, waiting on him with a patience that whispered of angels and an end to shadows.

Finally she spoke. "Hello, my poor, shrinking darling, how still you be." Softly she went over and smoothed his wax-like forehead and pulled her fingers through the smudge of his pale hair. He opened his burned-out eyes. "What angel has come to haunt me?"

She leaned over and kissed him. "Not engel, love, voman."

"Give me your hand."

She shoved her hand into his, surprised at the strength of his grasp, her free hand smoothing the sheet over his gaunt, skeletal frame. "You be stronger today!"

"Feel like giving Fontane some competition."

She laughed and lifted his hand high. "Yay!" she trilled.

But his face grew somber as once again Urliss read the message in his eyes. Shall we prolong this? God forbid, let us put it behind us as decently as possible. "How're the dogs?" he asked, annoyed that his voice was raspy.

"Oh, dey're fine. Kip took dem to hunt last evening; de grouse are everywhere."

"Good." Pleasure illuminated the dry, shiny skin of his face. As so many times before, a long look passed between them. "You're the cutest Norwegian in the county," he said. And after a minute he added, "I'd like to see the boys. Understand Ethan's growing a beard now that he's home."

"Does not look bad, and a good ting, for I cannot do much vid him."

Dow snorted. "Patronizing young devil, ain't he?"

"He smarter dan all of us now."

"They'll do a job on him, make him reactionary. He'll learn that those like myself who would preserve our heritage are extremists, warmongers, nonintellectual—"

"Whoa," Urliss laughed and put a finger lightly over his lips. "He is good boy, don't you vorry; he knows you be a good man."

Dow closed his eyes and smiled. "Well, I want to see them today. I'm up to it. Sometimes when Kip has been here I haven't been alert. Everything gets remote."

But John came first and Urliss hesitated before asking Dow if he should come in. Drawing on her learned pose of "now let's be calm and very pleasant," she dropped herself onto the chair's edge and soothed Dow's shaggy hair. "John Johnson has come. Do you feel up to him, or shall he come back anoder time?"

" 'Course I'll see him. Good of him to come." He studied her from under bushy brows and then he smiled. He did not add, "for old times' sake," or "because the ties of the land should be stronger than ideologies." Nor did he say, "I want to think that when I'm gone this old breach will heal till it's less than a little foolishness, a slight misunderstanding among friends." But probably it was all of these reasons lumped together.

A sense of dread gnawed at Urliss. She wanted to protest; she *should* protest. Dow was not up to this; how poor he looked suddenly—no he was not up to it. She pressed her trembling hands into a taut little ball and said, "My goodness, is time nurse gave you a shot."

He shook his head. "Not yet, not till tonight."

So Urliss looked on while the two met—the half-breed with his craggy, kind face and fathomless eyes, and her darling, wasted and pale, the ghost of the great man whom John had known.

"Well, John," Dow smiled at John's warm, unrelenting gaze. Solemnly they studied each other.

All those years, John was thinking sadly, they had been friends of a sort, knitted together through their mutual understanding of the call of the prairie—a call which touched the drives and hungers of their own spirits. How chill was the wind that had driven them apart.

"Glad you came," Dow said. "Good to see you, sit down. The work lettin' up a little, is it?"

"Up or down, I forget which," John chuckled, shaking the baron's hand as he sank into a chair that Urliss had placed on the far side of her rocker.

"Nasty weather," Dow grunted. "The grain just squats there." He stared at the big field of pale green through the window.

"When that wicked breeze lets up it'll tear away," John reassured him.

"Did you come to pray over me, John? To speak words of absolution?" Dow teased him. "Or maybe you want to reassure me that the millennium is about to break on this poor nation."

John chose his words cautiously. "I believe God will give

peace in answer to the prayers of His people if we are obedient to the principles of His love."

Dow wagged his head and grinned slightly. "Y'know, John, you might've convinced me that your religion had some merit if you hadn't wanted to make a mealy-mouthed doormat out of me!"

John leaned forward earnestly. "People of all sorts of political persuasions believe in Jesus Christ—trust their lives to Him. Dow, don't turn Him away because my political views aren't the same as yours."

Dow studied John, his eyes glinting feverishly. "You're a cunning fellow, John, charming the air you breathe with nosegays for your cause, so amiable and sincere that even the rabble come around, all suddenly eager to join your church and do away with injustice forever." He paused, gathering a fresh breath himself.

"So folks of many persuasions love the same God, eh?" he said, thinking to conquer him now. "The God of many faces, eh? Just how inconsistent is He? He helps you, a socialist, to show us all how to give away our wealth and reputations while old Griffith down the road is a capitalist of the original order, rich as Croesus, and thinks he's God's favored nephew, spouting his religion as ardently as you."

Again Dow grunted. For a minute they were silent, and then they both started to talk at once. They laughed and Urliss laughed also, a short sound of relief. "Go ahead," Dow commanded.

"Dow," John said gently, "I came to pay my respect to you. I want you to know I feel you're a rare and good man. I apologize for not being the neighbor I should've sometimes."

Dow looked surprised. "Why, thank you, John." A minute later he added stiffly, "You're a good man in spite of bein' a dreamer."

John's face shone with pleasure. "We should've stressed the things we had in common. We'd've been better off."

"No doubt. Well, I haven't heard a lick of news in days; Urliss keeps my mind as dark as the room." Irritation crept into his voice. "So what's happening, John? Are the bureaucrats still pretending to run this country? Has anyone discovered a cure for the common cold?"

"Newspapers don't change much from day to day. But there

does seem to be a strong conservative trend, at least in the grass-roots. The language of their cause is so strong though—don't know whether to cheer or worry."

"Fat chance a good conservative will get the helm in this country today." Garstin grimaced as pain bit through him. He regained his breath. "And what do *you* purpose as a solution to the world's problems? Now it seems to me your God ought to impress His followers as to which position is correct, yours or His. I'm a lot closer to Griffin," he added, "selfish old goat that he is. Maybe he's a bit of a hypocrite, but I respect him for the self-made patriot that he is. He'd fight to the death for Old Glory and a hard day's work. The world you're bringing in I'd not fit into at all."

Emoting a tender and eager spirit, John leaned forward. "Well, how could you know about that world, Dow? It's never existed since Adam fell, never been given a fair trial. I tell you that such a world where the Spirit of God could move through the obedient love of His people would be the greatest system any man has ever dared dream about. There's a greater power than the atom bomb here, Dow. It's the power of the Lord's people being pure vessels for the Holy Spirit. It's then you'd see armies stopped in their tracks, the wicked rendered impotent, the starving fed, and the earth as clean as a daisy in the first morning."

Dow closed his eyes. "You're talkin' riddles again, John."

"I'm not a politician, Dow. Politics has been the church's undoing through the centuries. Instead of being the spiritual force God called it to be, it has often raised its fist like a worldly power. If it would do Christ's work, praying with the fervor of broken, loving hearts, the world would come to Him." He added intensely, "Do you get the picture, Dow? An army of little Christs full of spiritual power to move the nations to God."

"Until you'd end up like Him, on a stake."

"But He's not on the stake anymore, Dow. He's alive, He lives in heaven and He lives in His people. Don't you see? It's through *us* He wants to work. Dow," he added, wanting him to understand, "that's why I lay down my arms. We Christians must bring life, not death."

"Your eyes are so glazed by the sun of idealism," Dow said bitterly, "that you can't possibly measure the cowardice in your position. You'd let this nation go to her doom while you called out, 'Thus saith the Lord!' to all the rabble, near and far. But in the end, they'd be your masters—*your* masters—and the masters of all those blind prisoners you were talking about saving. You'd seal the doom of the whole free world. By George, I can't believe it!"

John looked troubled. It was clear that he had not reached Dow with his vision of a powerful God who could be trusted.

"What, besides robbing the honest and deceiving the gullible, has your church accomplished in your lifetime, John?" Dow suddenly demanded.

John said patiently, "If you'd stick to facts just once, instead of going off half-cocked, maybe you could catch a glimpse of Christ."

"Facts! Facts? By George, I've never heard you come up with a fact yet! I can't tolerate such divine stupidity, Johnson. You're crazy as a bobcat in a turpentine barrel!" Dow rose halfway up on his elbow. "If there's a picnic up yonder, you and your goody two-shoes breed should be roasted at the fire." He lapsed into a fit of coughing.

"Stop, oh, stop," Urliss urged, her face gone white and fearful. "John, you must not argue vid Dow, you hear? He too sick to be upset such like dis!"

"I'm truly sorry, Miss Peterson. Dow, you old turnip, you heard the lady, no fightin'." but John's face was strained with distress and shame and had paled visibly.

"—senseless for you and me to smoke the pipe, John. There's no reasoning with you. So I want you to go away! And don't come back," Dow ordered through a throat fogged by spasm.

John stood up slowly, as if he could not believe his words. "Dow," he begged, "don't send me out like this. I beg you, let's say a warm farewell."

"Better 'n you deserve, at that." A muscle twitched fiercely in his cheek, into which some color had come.

"I should've known better. I only wanted you to see the kingdom of God, Dow—the love Christ has for you." He stood awkwardly, as if he would say more, as if he hoped Dow would forgive him. But in the long silence he turned slowly toward the door.

After he had left, Urliss exclaimed, "You hurt him, Dow!"

"Hurt him! That fool, it's like talking to a lot of stone!"

Urliss continued to stare at him in sad amazement. "You not yourself, Dow. Someting has hold of you."

"A sense of justified outrage has hold of me. John's no better than a traitor. We ought to send him to Russia!"

"He is good man," Urliss defended him, "veder you agree vid him or not."

Dow was thoughtful for a moment. "Johnson calls himself a Christian, but he's a socialist, a monstrous dreamer with schemes for peace by surrender!" He trembled violently.

"Please, darling, I never see you upset so; please be still!"

Dow's eyelids dropped and the room grew quiet. After a while he said, "What kind of fool am I to get so stirred up about the nation till it becomes a storm in me that never stops breaking? I'm almost done here, so what difference does it make? Still, I'll go out raving against the likes of Marx and Johnson."

"Dere now," she moved to smooth the pleat in his wild thatch of hair. "You care because you love, dat is vhy." Her speech was as much an attempt to clear her own perspective as it was to reassure him, but even as the words came, a sort of misgiving bewitched her.

He smiled at her, his anger and despair going away. He opened his eyes to say, "You're the cutest Norwegian in Ordlow County!"

When Kip and Ethan arrived Urliss met them at the door. "Dow vants you now. Ah, Kip, your hands are black vid grease. Did you not vash? And tuck in your shirt, den come." She herded them in front of her anxiously. "Now remember," she whispered to Ethan, "yust be natural."

"Is he better?" Ethan inquired, trying to tip-toe quietly.

"He is having a good day."

Inside the den the brothers blinked at the obscure gloom, and Ethan ignored Urliss's firm prodding hands on his back. "Dow?" his voice sounded uncertain and boyish.

"Hi, there, hi, there," a smile lighted the depressed planes of Dow's face. "Come in and tell me what you've been up to." As Kip moved to stand beside the bed, the baron gazed at him with sunken, feverish eyes. "You're filling out, too, Kip. Let me look at you. He'll be a big man, Urliss."

Urliss nodded and smiled.

" 'lo, Dow." Ethan took his outstretched hand. "Sure miss you."

"Getting ready to brand, are you?"

"Next week."

"Tell us about school. You're satisfied?"

"It's all right. I like it fine." His voice trailed off.

"Are they teaching you fables or the real stuff?"

"They get their licks in for both."

Dow's expression was genial. "You'll make a good lawyer," he decided.

"I hope so, thanks."

"Many have come to pay respect," Urliss announced proudly, "ah, I should have wrote down names."

"No need," Dow reassured her.

"And six hippies from commune brought vegetable soup."

"So they're still around," Dow observed mildly.

"Some are building the new rest home. Dey vork hard, no pay."

Dow remarked drily that it "must've been a lot of soup if it took six of them to bring it," and the boys laughed with relief.

"Let's have some light, Urliss. Open the curtains wide; by George, it's a dungeon in here. Ah, that's better, look at that grain grow, needs a drink, though." In the light, Garstin's face was waxen and pale, his powerful arms shrunken away thin as a young girl's where they protruded from his pajama tops. The sight made Ethan cringe. He is a brave man, he thought. There is nothing so sad in all the world as seeing a strong, handsome man shriveling up and helpless as a baby. "We better go," he said uncertainly, "we can come again tomorrow."

"Why, you just came," Dow protested.

"Is enough," Urliss agreed. "Dey vill come back."

"All right," Dow sighed, "come back then, good-bye."

"Good-bye," they said. "Good-bye, Dow." Again they permitted Urliss to usher them.

Outside Ethan said, "I don't believe that's Dow Garstin. I think somebody played a dirty trick on us." He punched his brother's arm angrily.

Kip's eyes glistened. "If only he knew Christ," he said brokenly. His concern for Dow's soul bordered on agony. Once he had opened up the Word to Dow, his face earnest and hopeful as he had read portions to the dying man. "Dow, do you believe in Jesus?" Kip had asked him.

"Sure do," Dow had answered. "Just like the Chinese believe in Buddha and Confucius."

Kip had whispered intensely, "Christ is *God!*"

"So aren't we all?" Dow had responded. "Don't we have divine stuff in us?"

"We strut around like it," Kip agreed. "But in Christ God became the Savior of this world."

"You're a fine lad, Kip, but don't waste your breath. I'll go out as I've lived, and my record will have to stand. Mistakes I've made, but I've clothed my days with honor. Beyond that, the Great Judge will take care of my life on the other side—if there is one."

But Kip could not dismiss the prospect of Dow's bleak and tragic fall into even deeper spiritual darkness with the passing of his physical life. His concern for him broke out in dark impressions and dreams.

Kip's new and anguished concern for Dow, for Ethan, for the community and even the entire world gave birth to terrible imaginings at times. The thought of a child being abused by a twisted parent or an old man wasting with disease and remorse or a prisoner huddled fearfully in a nest of dirty rags made him howl with grief inside his head. His soul felt it all—the blows to his body, the mental anguish, the torment of spirit. Often he would run through the fields, sobbing through his hands, bending over double with the hurting of it all. His embrace of the Savior had aroused a new awareness of a desperate world.

John told him, "Your anguish for suffering souls is the cross Christ asks us to help Him carry. When those impressions come to you, cry out in intercessory prayer; God generates power through the prayers of His children to lift the world into His love."

So now, when Dow and others came to his mind, Kip immediately cried out to God and was overcome by an awareness of God's own great heart crying with Kip and through him.

"If only Dow knew Christ," he later repeated to Ethan who compressed his lips and said bitterly, "Oh, yeah, that'd make everything straight up."

That evening when Kip returned to relieve Urliss from sitting with Dow, there was an ambulance parked in the yard and they were bringing the baron out on a stretcher, his body covered with a light blanket. Urliss and the nurse climbed into the vehicle, also. It was like a silent movie with no one saying a word, no one noticing Kip at all. When the long limousine turned into the lane, the lights shone fully on him like two bulbous eyes blinking at his frozen face and passing on.

Kip went to the back door and let himself into the kitchen. The whole house was lit up as if it were waiting for guests. He clomped heavily down the long hall. The door to Dow's den was ajar and Kip pushed it open further, exposing a rumpled bed and the stark desk and heavy drapes. Medicine bottles crowded the top of the commode.

The effervescent smell of antiseptic still lingered. Trance like, he crossed over to the bed. The impression of Dow's great head still dented the pillow and for a long time he stared down at that faint cleft, remembering the proud, high look of him, the fineness and integrity in his bearing, remembering his mane of pale hair blowing in the wind as he sat astride Fontane loping over the grasslands. Impulsively he knelt down and pressed his own face into the cleft, sniffing the vague odor of hair creme and camphor. "God," he groaned, "don't let him go out into the dark."

11

Passing Over

The night wears wan,
Coldness comes with dawn,
I must go on. . . .

WHEN ETHAN had arrived home for summer vacation, the first tender fringe of grain was stealing over the fields like green shag rugs stretched from hill to swale and back again, and he had torn into the work with a frenzy. He and Kip were inseparable, working the fields together, fencing together, riding herd together. Ethan and Melanie were engaged now, and it seemed to the brothers that all the past seasons were falling before their eyes like a parade of dominoes and this summer would mark the end of something, the end of an interdependence that would shift radically as Ethan married and prepared for his own vocation. A gentle force seemed to animate all the endearing qualities of Kip's personality so that he was more sense-tuned to Ethan than ever before.

Sometimes they played together, wrestling and strong-arm testing and holding skirmishes at the water trough. But mostly they wore themselves out like ants building a kingdom. When they weren't cleaning stables or pounding a bent drill, they were getting ready for the next round of field work following a short night of heavy sleep.

Ethan often talked about Melanie, confiding his plans and deepest feelings. "Man, she has power over me," he confessed to his brother more than once. "The first six months I knew her, I couldn't remember my own name."

"I can believe it. I had a crush on her myself." Kip averted his gaze, suddenly self-conscious with the memory of that terrible and ecstatic time.

Ethan grinned. "Can't blame you for that."

"You can laugh, but I went through a lot of hell over it. She's your girl and I got this crush on her and felt like Judas. Y'know, that's what drove me to Christ."

"I'll be danged." Ethan's grin broadened visibly. "So that's what made a religious nut out of you." He studied his brother with open amusement. Kip was full of all the pesky fevers of the new convert, taking off in all directions at once in his effort to bring the world to Christ, and Ethan liked to topple him from his pulpit by teasing him.

Now, as they were nearing town, Ethan rolled down the window of the truck and started shouting warnings at the passersby. "Run for cover! Here comes the Jesus boy, and he's after you."

"Aw, cut it out," Kip said good-naturedly.

But Ethan was enjoying himself. "Yessiree, friends and neighbors, if you like your booze and a little fun in the backyard, ya' better hide away quick or you're apt to lose it all. Saint Kip is about to set upon you poor, unsuspecting sinners with his tracts and Bibles, and he's as persuasive as a sweet girl in pink bloomers. . . ." Already some of their neighbors were crossing to the other side of the street from where Kip was parking the truck, and Ethan was cracking up with laughter.

"Smart mouth," Kip muttered before slamming the door and making his way down the street.

Later, as they rode home Kip started singing some scripture choruses which set Ethan's teeth on edge worse than his testimonials. "Anybody ever tell you that you can't carry a tune in a barrel!" he demanded. "And those dumb songs remind me of the crazies on John's place."

But Kip did not seem to mind the razzing. He went on singing for a few minutes, stomping his feet and snapping his fingers and carrying on, Ethan said, "like a freak in a bear trap."

But in spite of his religious spinoff and aggravating testimonials, Kip had come into some puzzling dimension of personality that made him seem old and wise, as if he understood things beyond his ken, a sort of listening quality that brought Ethan up short from time to time in an eye-narrowing wonder at "what the Sam Hill was going on."

Still he jeered at his brother, "As big as this universe is, what makes you think you have the corner on truth? Are you any better than the disciple of Zen or Confucius?" And when Kip would have replied, he shouted him down. "Every dog worries his own bone. You carry your bag, I'll tote mine. Life is complicated enough without clobbering it up with a lot of unprovable theories."

Ethan pitied people who submitted their ego to a cause or deity that left them barren in self-realization. "You're just naturally humble, Kip," he told him kindly. "I'm too mean to sing my swan song for a God who demands first rights on my pride!"

He was surprised, though, that his younger brother had gotten close to Dow. Whenever the dying man crept into their speech, Kip grew agitated with pity and often wept openly. Every evening, no matter how late the hour, he showered and dressed in fresh clothes and went over to sit with his friend.

Urliss, too, spent so much time with Dow that the Kettrie home was left to gloom and cobwebs and warmed-over stew, against all of which Ethan was grudgingly pitting his smarts in learning the basics of boiling and frying and scouring.

"They were going to get married," Kip told him.

Ethan whistled. "That might've taken some of the orneriness outta Urliss." He smiled, but Kip looked so solemn he added, "Naw, I'm sorrier than you know. The poor mermaid. I wonder if she's just a loser."

"He wants so bad to die," Kip said, "but he just keeps hangin' on. There must be a reason for it," he added.

"There doesn't have to be a reason for everything," Ethan said evenly. "If God cared as much as you want him to, Dow'd be long gone."

Kip's eyes were wet. "Every night I pray he'll be released and that his soul will be ready."

They had just started working over the summer fallow the second time when Dow started sinking fast and was taken a second time to Ordlow County Hospital. "He won't be happy dying away from his land," Kip said.

"They'll keep him drugged. He won't know the difference," Ethan reassured him.

But Kip headed out for the commune to visit Anna. Even over her reluctance they had become friends. Often Kip brought her to the ranch so they could ride horses. Both of them would chatter and laugh and discuss their faith as they moved into the comfort of their blooming friendship. Sitting easy in their saddles they would ride over old trails and around the dams and ponds and up onto the high knolls where they could stop and look away to the Reservation and the town no bigger than a match stick, letting the wind slap at them.

One day Anna said, "It's never far from my mind that the world is running scared out there, and we have this big prairie wrapped around us like a security blanket." They had drawn up by a reservoir to let the horses drink and a sweet yearning came to Anna's face. "Oh, Kip, if only we could bring all the hurting people here where the healing power of the Holy Spirit is so strong."

Kip grew excited. "I know what you're saying. Man, how I sense His presence as I roam around. He's lonesome, I think, looking for people to love. There's not many around. You think so, Anna? You think He's looking for companionship in this big country?"

"I sure do." Letting the horse's reins fall around the saddle horn, she cupped her hands around her mouth and called out, "Give me your ghettos and poor, your broken and bruised, your old and forsaken. Come to the prairie, come to Jesus. He's here with His wind to dry your wounds, His sun to warm your hearts. . . ."

"If I were rich," Kip said, "if I owned the ranch free and clear, I'd like to share it with the poor. I'd like to sign it over to the Lord as sort of a resting place for some of His needy souls."

Anna was moved. "You would, Kip. You're a rare and lovely man." Her lips trembled and she brushed angrily at sudden tears.

"I'm entering in to the spirit of what you Helpers are trying to say with your lives, that's all. Once Christ gets a hold on you, you lose your desire for building your own kingdom. You see the world with a whole new outlook," he went on with a sort of surprise as if in defining this change of heart vocally he was coming to a fresh awareness of its dimension. "Your main ambition becomes your desire to bring the world to God—or bring Him to the world, however you want to put it. And that's how you start looking at your own life, not 'what can I *get*?' but 'what can I *give*?' "

"That's right, Kip, oh, that's right." Anna was crying openly now. They both laughed with the joy of it all.

But then Kip grew sober and pensive. "I go to church with John, you know, Anna. It speaks to my needs. We're a family there. I wish you'd visit with me sometime.

"Now, I don't want to hurt your feelings, Anna, but there are a lot of folks, Christian and otherwise, living off the strength of the church's good influence but knocking her down by taking pot shots one way or another and refusing to support her in any way. I wonder where Christianity would be today if it wasn't for the organized church."

"Probably a lot further ahead," Anna bristled. "Probably the whole world would have come in by now."

"That's pretty dumb, and you should know it."

"Well, when the church starts living like a real servant of Jesus Christ, then we'll all go in."

"That's plumb snooty if you ask me. The church is made up of people like you and me, and we're each at different stages of growth and understanding, so we're not all doing the right things all the time. The church is for believers, Anna, believers who need lifting and loving just like the helpers at your community do."

Anna nodded. "True enough, but the church is called to be responsible, to be a humble servant to the world, not to bask in the pleasure of being God's chosen people. Kip, they're the ones who are often arrogant, taking all the goodies while the world starves!"

"You're an idealist, Anna, so is Brother Ben. You've got to come to terms with reality, deal with things the way they are, not like they might be if everyone were properly focused on Christ twenty-four hours a day. Obviously, they should be, but it's a growing process, little girl, and in the meantime the church needs the same vision and willingness to sacrifice that you and the brothers have. Don't you see that you should get inside, be a good example? Help the church grow through your love and gentleness. Then you'd be effective for Christ instead of an embarrassment, making everyone uneasy."

"So we're an embarrassment." Anna fought sudden tears.

"You know you are; Christians want to be kind, but you shake the dust off your feet."

"That's not true," Anna was trying to hide her hurt. She chewed thoughtfully at her lip. "I don't want to argue with you, Kip."

He grinned. "Then don't. Come to church with me Sunday morning."

She flashed a tight smile at him and loped away, heading back toward the barn.

"You've made it tough for John, too," he called after her as he raced Dierdre to catch up.

When they reached the stable, Anna quickly dismounted and began loosing the cinch strap with trembling fingers.

"Anna." Kip's voice was husky and gentle as he drew up beside her and slid off Dierdre, putting his arm around Anna's waist all at once. Tenderly he turned her stiffening body around and held her, feeling the lean, sweet warmth of her, as she, for a fleeting moment, relaxed. Then she struck at him and broke into tears and started running away. "I am not for you, leave me alone; don't come near me again!" she yelled over her shoulder, fleeing like a young deer through the field that led to Garstin's ranch.

"Anna, you silly girl, come back here!" Kip shouted, but she kept on running. Impatient and suddenly angry, he mounted his mare once more and chased after her, letting her run until she was worn out and her breath came in great, heaving gulps. Getting down, he hoisted her into Dierdre's saddle. After slapping the horse's rump he instructed Anna to "ride on home" while he himself turned back to the barn, disappointment causing his face to go set and stony. Let 'er go, then, he said to himself. He wouldn't bother her again.

Once more Kip threw himself into the endless work of the ranch, giving an assist occasionally to John who, in turn, directed the hired men at the Garstin ranch.

In his spiritual life Kip was recognizing a sort of dry wilderness place in his walk. He missed the lovely sense of Christ's presence and though he went doggedly ahead on blind faith, reading the Word, praying and going to church, he often pelted heaven with questions about the way God was running things. The events and circumstances of his own life were a disappointment and the concern for souls dying without Christ was a growing burden to him until he was often close to tears.

Independence Day broke hot and sticky, full of forebodings. Shoving his chair back from the breakfast table with the shrill clamor of the phone, Kip seemed to sense that Dow was crossing over the last hill. On the other end of the line Urliss said, "Kom," in a voice both strong and stumbling. He put the phone down very carefully, jotted a note for Ethan who was playing cowboy somewhere in the north range, grabbed up his wallet and flew to the pickup.

The sky grew dark as thunder clouds roared across the country, overturning the trough of heaven with a great gush of water. But by the time Kip reached Ordlow the sun was once again a fat, round ball of fire and the annual Fourth-of-July parade was forming rank for its winding street pageant. Proud ranchers marshalled their finest horses for bearing the colors proudly at the lead. The band marched to Semper Fidelis, and a long line of veterans and civic-minded figures moved with their floats onto Main Street.

At the hospital Kip could smell hypocrisy all over the place. Sunshine and chatting nurses with their brisk, busy movements were some sort of camouflage, he thought. There should be a message carved over the archway reading, "Here is the final battle, the last shuddering cry of man in his flesh." A dying man should know that the white-frocked nurses and multi-masked visitors are *aware* that he's crossing over. He should feel their *respect*. He thought about how people skimmed over life like a skater on the pond, covering its holiness with a lot of froth and frenzy while deep down there was both the joy cloud and the wailing wall. In Kip's opinion the essence and the reality of *being* needed to be uncovered and released so a person could be a child of freedom and light instead of a dim-witted swamp man moving around *getting* and *doing* and not making too much sense of the reason for it all. He prayed, "Christ, it all comes together in you. If only everyone could see it!" With a sense of reverence he moved into room 310.

Through the cavernous funnels of his laboring mind, Dow heard the muted roll of drums announcing that the parade was coming, and old, tattered scenes came to play. High over the beads of her proud-stepping soldiers were the colors of America, his home and sweet mother. "Salute the flag, good men and patriots, ah, salute the flag. America will be clean and proud and strong forever!" Now run, run and follow the parade. Feel the fever of the rattling drums, throw your cap in the air. . . ."

But what was this? The parade was fading away, and kingdoms were rising like little fires from black holes. Dow saw the fires burn out like candles in a strong wind, saw them fall away to ashes, saw America rise as a quick, bright campfire in a black thicket with many passing strangers warming their hands over her. And then he saw the smoke of her billow like an umbrella and the fire became a smudge, and his heart grew heavy with despair. But at the center of the smudge was a tiny light, so white and fierce that it hurt Dow's eyes to look at it. He watched that light mushroom, ever so slowly, saw it flicker with threatened extinction time after time, but finally become an exceeding great light overpowering all the campfires, growing larger and greater until it touched the sky and covered the stars and the moon and even the sun.

The brightness was so intense now that Dow had to strain his vision and little drops of sweat fell from his brow. Then he closed his eyes and leaned back, knowing that he had just seen something awful and profound, the blazing cross of the kingdom of lights, the kingdom of God. He strained to bring back the vision that had come and gone as the meaning of it swept over him. The man of glory, the Creator, had come to fall upon His rebel world, hugging it all to His great bosom—the sobbing, groaning, dying masses. He had stretched himself out with brokenness and tears, pouring out His life's blood for them all.

So you are Christ! Astonishment welled up within him and then gave way to dark remorse for his own ignorance and pride and his bitter rejection of that One who was the reason for all his questing search after perfection. He saw himself now as unbending, without true pity. He had given his life to the pursuit of lesser, passing things. You were worthy of all my allegiance, he thought.

He turned feverishly, losing himself in a gripping sorrow.

"I'm dying." Truth became brutal in its clarity. Regret for what he had missed crouched like a weeping dream on his conscience and filled his soul, forming thick words under his tongue.

Urliss, seeing his lips move, bent close. Opening his eyes to her sweet, strained face, he knew that the most lovely thing he had ever experienced was her committed love spreading out her soul like a blanket to cover him. He tried desperately to soothe what he had hurt. He smiled, a crooked tender smile, the more pitiable because it exposed rather than covered the pathos of his feeling. "Precious." To his knowledge he had never used the word before, and it fell in a guttural scratch from his lips with some surprise to himself. But he repeated laboriously, "Precious, you."

Urliss halted her hand that had started to caress him and stared with uncomprehending eyes.

On the other side of Dow, Kip gripped his hand and started to pray, his throat hurting with unspoken grief. "Jesus," he prayed for the hundredth time, "give him light."

Over the fog filling his throat Dow tried to speak. "Good boy," he struggled to say, "good . . . boy." Now the great, blinding light flooded the room, hurting his eyes. "Jesus," he whispered.

And Kip and Urliss knew that Someone had come, cutting across their anguish like a soft, soothing hand. They recognized the presence of Christ. He was here, so pervasive and full of tender love that they wept unashamedly.

12

The Rage of August

While lanterns shattered across His ceiling
you learned God's wrath;
and shook like the rattling wind,
waiting, waiting for hell.

ON THE DAY that Dow Garstin's ashes were flung like
broadcast seed over his fields, a hot, dry wind moaned through
the coulees. Once more it was August and the harvest grains were
bleached and brittle. Ethan maneuvered his father's old combine
through the smallest field, while Kip drove the truck, catching
loads of grain on the run. The wheat yielded plump, hard kernels
like gold nuggets and everywhere the mood was exultant.

Again Urliss moved from table to stove in the Kettrie house, a
sort of ennui engulfing her as she stood motionless, staring out
the window at the sea of rolling land going on forever. She muttered in sad little hums from time to time. Her face contorted
with tears.

But she kneaded bread with her old relish. Plop! went her
fist. Plop, plop, plop! "Vun ting . . ." Plop! ". . . I vill not. . ."
Plop! "put up vid . . . is dirt carried into de house! All dat vheat
scattered on de floor is dirt from pockets by toughtless boys and
hired hand!" Plop, plop!

Dow had given half of his holdings to her, the other part—
that which joined Shellydown for five miles across—to Kip and
Ethan. "You're a big landowner now," Ethan had said softly to
Urliss after Dow's lawyer had explained how the sick man had
transferred title to them before his death. A short, humorless
laugh from Urliss conveyed the bitter irony of wealth without
pleasure. "Vy, Dow," she wondered once through the hot, blow-

155

ing winds that threw her plea back onto her pale, trembling lips, "vy I should stay in dis god-forsaken vilderness and tend your flocks vhile I die? Herre Gud, I vill not! I vill sell every barn and pebble and use money for fine, luxury life, wisit home in Norvay vearing clothes of qveen, have home on ocean, chauffeur for big car!" She quivered with anger and frustration.

But slowly she permitted herself to be coaxed to little visits to the town she loved, responding with grateful, if mechanical, friendliness to kind overtures from friends there. It was through the love of the people and through the congregation sounding their liturgical antiphonies in the dome-ceilinged Lutheran church that she might find her spirit again, she thought, comforted by the traditions of her childhood.

One day she tucked away the diamond that Dow had placed on her finger, shutting the lid of a tiny chest on its glorious bevels, crackling through white ice. Suddenly she knew she would have preferred a different stone, something rosy and warm.

"Maybe I give de ring to Kip vun day, for his bride," she murmured. But then she felled the thought with a mighty blow because a sinking sadness captured her mind. What girl could be good enough for her poor *foreldrelos*, her tender orphan, her *engel* boy? "None of dose self-centered, unchaste scalavags, so common nowadays," she vowed. The girl for Kip must be gentle and virtuous and very loving and loyal. Lord Gud, did they not make such creatures in this violent, sensual land?

Just so it was Kip who cried to her spirit, piercing it with new life as he called to the mother in her. She looked after him anxiously, softly hounding his steps with cold juice and a change of socks and forty winks after lunch, straining for glimpses of him as he worked the fields. Often she went to the door and, shielding her eyes from the pitiless sun, looked for a trace of that one whom she loved, whom her soul yearned over. Vat is it? she asked the sky, so calm and blue it seemed to be winking at her. Vat is dis I feel? Some devil chasing my darling *engel* boy? And for him she would stay on in the big country.

One day in late August a hush fell over the land with a bright spangled haze that hung like a canopy over the fields so that the harvest workers kept a wary eye peeled for hail clouds. At twilight sheets of light flashed like neon over the horizon and, when

full dark came, a ground lightning winnowed in with fiery, darting tongues licking the grass. In no time swirls of smoke and
flame erupted on the skyline and half the men on the breeches
took off to fight the prairie fire. The rest of the ranchers stayed
home to guard their own and their neighbor's land with tanks of
water mounted on their trucks, laboring under the ominous
threat to the crops with redoubled efforts to get their grain in.

The next day after lunch Kip took a load of wheat to town,
keeping the truck windows rolled down so the hot, oppressive air
could slap him and keep him alert. The work load that had grown
to include a portion of the Garstin spread had sloughed off his energy so that when he sat still for any length of time he grew
groggy.

On his way home he spied some of his commune friends working in their cornfield and he honked the horn and waved. Only
that morning he had learned through John that they were talking
about breaking camp because they weren't making it. He wondered about Anna, where she would go, what would become of
her. Often when he stopped by he saw her, but only once had she
turned to fully look at him with that same poignant expression
that had struck him at their very first encounter. The other times
she had bowed her head and slipped away as if she wanted to
hide from him. "Wonder what ails her," he muttered. "Maybe
my barn-raising for the church at our last discussion—thinks
she's too good to associate with us steeple chasers." But he felt
sick at heart, knowing that her behavior went deeper than that.
Looking back on it he saw that she had never really been at ease
with him, and he could not understand it because he sensed that
she really liked him.

In mid-afternoon Kip moved a load of wheat from the south
field to the granary, parked the truck and went to the house
where he drank a pitcher of lemonade and wolfed down two
peaches. Urliss had left for Ordlow where she had agreed to play
hostess for Ladies' Aid, and the house was quiet but for the whir-
ring window-cooler that enticed him to stretch out on the living
room rug where the cool air might restore his energy. In no time
at all he fell asleep.

When he wakened, his hair still clung in moist little cowls to
his forehead and he was weak as a kitten. Staggering groggily

back to the kitchen, he gulped another glass of lemonade, flipped his cap back onto his head and trudged lazily outdoors. The air was damp and thick, oppressive like a wet blanket. The sight in the great field east of the buildings congealed his brain so that he was frozen onto the stoop. It seemed the whole world was ablaze.

In near panic he started off in several directions at once— toward the phone, toward the pickup, and finally toward the tractor with growing purpose and determination. Little tremors spurted up and down the cables of his brain, jerking at his fingers so that it was an effort to back up the old tractor to the oneway disc harrow and hitch them together. His sense of timing was so rattled—that it seemed the whole ranch might burn up before he could do a thing about it. In high gear he raced to the fire, observing as he drew closer that the inferno was still contained on the grassland. It had not yet reached the wheat field which would claim the heaviest yield.

The only thing Kip knew to do was to harrow a wedge around the grain to the place where it joined a huge strip of summer fallow, clinging to the hope that the air would remain still so that the flames would not leap the plowed-under stalks.

In order for the blades to bite deep enough into the hard turf, Kip had to move at the tractor's lowest speed. With an eye cast desperately on the spreading blaze, he thought what a grim and ugly thing it was, leaping and spewing like some primeval monster driven by wicked lust to devour all the poor green and gold of the sweet land. It was spreading faster than he had judged, racing now toward the end of the field, gaining on him so that he felt helpless, like another thin, brittle stalk in the monster's path. He shoved at the gears, letting the tractor groan and shudder as it labored to rip the disc through the matted grain.

Suddenly he caught sight of Ethan's pickup bounding toward him. Relief felled his tension and fears; everything would be all right now. Ethan was coming. He turned slightly to hail him.

At that moment the discs at the edge of the grazing ground caught a half-buried boulder and the whole rig tipped over. Though Kip felt it go and tried to jump clear, he was hurled to the ground and his legs were pinned under the tractor, going from incredible pain to total numbness.

Stunned and in shock he felt Ethan's arms around him, pulling, pulling until they were both wringing wet and worn out. "C'mon," his brother kept saying, between gasping breath and tugs, "c'mon now, little brother, c'mon." He felt his brother's breath, warm and sweet on his face, coming now in tearing sobs.

"Y'need to chop my legs off. Could you do that, Ethan? Get the ax and chop them off right there, below my hips. . . ."

With his bare hands Ethan was clawing out a hollow in the thatched floor of earth in order to pull Kip's legs through. Although it all seemed to be happening through shadows on a far-off screen, Kip felt his mind become sharp and clear, saw the wall of smoke-tressed flames moving in, saw the sparks flying like cloven tongues, saw the gas slowly trickling from the tank into the glistening grasses like a busy little stream. It was a matter of minutes until he would be gone. The knowledge struck him with only passing surprise. A great calm settled on him. "Get outta here!" he yelled at his brother.

Ethan had raised half way up from his crouch where he was still laboring to claw a pit for Kip's legs, coughing and wheezing through lips dried with smoke and heat. A wild desperation had captured him so he did not appear to be himself at all but rather some mad creature fresh loosed from cage and chain. "Get out!" Kip yelled again, his voice shrill.

But again Ethan grabbed Kip's torso and began the senseless tugging.

"This whole rig's gonna blow, you idiot!" Kip screamed. "Stand back!"

"By God, I won't!" Ethan threw himself down beside him, hugging him frantically. "I won't leave you!"

Mustering a strength that came from somewhere beyond himself, Kip heaved against him, leading with his arms. "You're making it hell for me! I can't stand it! You go for us both, y'hear? Get, get back!" And then he added, gently, "Quick, kiss me good-bye."

His skin dry as an onion, mouth open and working with bewildered horror, Ethan raised himself to his knees and cradled his brother's face in his hands. Whimpering sounds issued from his throat as he kissed his forehead, his bony face, then he rocked onto his toes in a hobbled stoop and backed away, his eyes begging through the growing curtain of smoke. He tried to scream but only bellows of air were expelled from his lungs. With bands clasped over his chest as if in awful pain and stooping yet, he whirled round and round across the field. Suddenly he stood erect and howled at the smoke-darkened sun, horrible animal sounds. "You, God!" he shouted over and over, shouting it still much later to a wind that came up strong from nowhere.

Kip heard him screaming and pity for him came and went. Staring through lurid smoke at the raging furnace bearing down on him, he focused upon what was coming with great dread and fear.

So this was how he would go out, in his own backyard, violently, with his brother screaming over there like a wounded animal. Sweat poured from his forehead into his eyes; he was cold and could not stop shivering. God, I'm scared of fire.

"Jesus?" His voice was piping, like a child's. "Jesus, put your arms around me." Just above him black clouds swooped so low he could almost touch them. Kip mistook them for great smudges of smoke. As one of the clouds raced downward he could see right into its eyes, a spinning white auger, boring down as an arm bared and full of saving fury. "Jesus!" he cried as the edge of the black funnel blew up in bits and pieces all around him. Hail began to splatter against the tractor.

Far to the north Urliss Peterson drove home from town at a furious speed. It had been a pleasant afternoon in the Ladies' Aid harvest bazaar. Everyone had agreed that her streudal was special. At the end of the refreshment time Reverend Olson had come by, tipping his straw hat at the door as he praised her cooking. "None for supper left," Urliss would tell the men triumphantly. "The streudal vas so good, dey took seconds and Reverend Olson tree or four, maybe."

It was hot and sultry and the air was heavy with the stench of prairie fires. A smear of black clouds lined the horizon ahead. Urliss drove with all the windows open, letting her hair blow in the wind that whipped her face and arms like a fan and carried the pungent odor of smoke.

Just ahead a cloud with a long thick tail came swooping down so low that it startled her. She slowed up and finally braked to a stop. There she sat spellbound as she watched the storm build.

The first cloud was poised so low she thought she could reach up and touch it. Even as she watched, other clouds came racing and swooping down to join it, forming a great black menace that was flung upward, the eye of the storm churning until it seemed she was strapped in the bowels of it. She could just imagine herself being hurtled from cloud to cloud as the thunder boomed and hawed against her ears. Minutes later she smelled rain and the air cooled abruptly. "Ah, it is hail," she murmured, "somevhere it has smashed some poor farmer's grain fields." She cast a worried look toward Shellydown. How black it was over there. "Gud, don't let dem lose de grain," she begged, still awed by what she had just observed in the formation of a powerful storm.

13

My God, My God

Cry, God, on my way to the cross
you made for me when you longed
after me and sang old earth songs
to my lonely ecstasy. . . .

THOSE FIRST WEEKS after Kip's accident, Urliss wept almost incessantly, her soul full of pity. Friends and neighbors found her distracted on the one hand, withdrawn to dark grief on the other. "He vill never valk again, poor Kip," she would shake her head and cry into her towel, "his fine legs crushed. . . ." To John, who was having a hard time handling his own sadness but making a valiant effort to comfort her, she said, "I see too much; in dis year I have see too much."

"God is making us all into His holy children," John replied gently.

"He is a Tyrant, dat Vun," she blazed with a passing flicker of her old thinking. "He has broke my spirit."

"You'll get it back," John assured her after a minute's silence.

"If den Herre Gud is making daughter outta me, like you say, if He vants I should be more like Him, it should be glad time."

"It will be."

"No, is fearful, ugly." Her shoulders began to shake and she cried aloud. Clumsily John sought to soothe her. "Life's no ride on the eiderdown, not for anybody. I know it well, but He's aiming at something greater than we can fancy, making us fit for responsibility in a time to come. Look to Him. He can make your heart sing, even in trouble."

Urliss turned away, sealing herself off from his attempts to comfort her while struggling with the thought of Kip going

162

through life crippled, his body twisting and laboring with even the most fragile demands.

"And remember," John remonstrated softly, "we should praise God every hour for the gift of Kip's life. That tornado and cloudburst was nothing short of a miracle. It's the talk of the country."

Urliss came back from her wanderings to rail at him. "Better he should have die, poor boy!" she blazed, sobbing.

She longed to be with Kip during his confinement in a Seattle hospital where there was a special trauma unit particularly suited to his injuries. And she resented Ethan for defying her, insisting as he had that he would support his own brother at this time and if either of them needed her he would let her know. As if Kip would not do a whole lot better if she were there each day to minister to his needs. But she fought through her jealousy, staying in the Kettrie home, unwilling yet to face the reality of living alone in Dow's house, writing letters to her angel boy, reminding him that as soon as Ethan had to leave for school she would be there.

Although she did not put it into so many words, even to herself, hers was an intuitive calling to mother Kip, and so great was her pity for him that she nailed the lid down on the coffin of the maiden in her who struggled to lift her golden head, and yearn after the dancing years, yearn for the lover she had never known. Winter was coming and she was fading away, almost used up, it seemed, as if she were older than her two-score-less-five years. The gaunt mobility of her face, mocked by the fading humor lines around her eyes that were soft and staring, suggested a sort of inertia so that when she came unexpectedly upon her reflection in some hanging mirror, she would hide her face and weep.

John was concerned for her. Sometimes she would feel his eyes on her. She would turn and, sure enough, there he would be, watching her, uneasy and awkward. "Are you praying for me, John?" she would tease. And he would smile and go away. But she drew on his strength and, despite their different views in matters of faith, an alliance sprang up between them and a warm intimacy was forged in their spirits. Though at times it was a shaky peace.

"Now you and religion take Kip from me, also." Urliss said with a moan. "Tick as tieves you be, you and him, and vid dose hippies at commune! Is *obsession*!" She glared at him, trembling with new tears. "I be all alone in dis mad vilderness of veed-smoking fools and fanatics!"

"You're not alone," John assured her. "If there's one thing you must know, it's that we care for you very much, Kip and I."

The ardor with which he spoke moved Urliss to contrition.

"Ah, my faith in de Lord grows on me, John. I am come to see I be not almost perfect as alvays I tink, but peevish and aloof, strong of dislikes. Most surely I regret dis now. Urliss must learn to comfort and love. Dis my Lord make me know."

John thought about that. "Yes," he consented, "yes, yes." He was glad for her confession. "Praise God, He is faithful to reveal us to ourselves here and there, so we can make a proper repentance." His pleasure grew so that he bounded to his feet. "Let's check the herds. Come with me."

But Urliss was slightly annoyed with John's hasty acknowledgment of her faults. "You go," she shrugged. "I stay."

After John had made a somewhat disappointed departure, Urliss grabbed her coat and hurried outdoors and down the lane to the mailbox. The sun was emerging from faltering clouds with jewel-like intensity, and she let her long-legged stride move freely, blinking at a gull winging and cawing low over her head.

There was no letter in the box and her disappointment was sharp. Neither of the boys was that thoughtful about writing to her. Ethan had called her twice in September, repeating bits of information about Kip and his treatment. When Urliss had insisted that he repeat everything slowly so she could write it down he had accommodated her with sighs and curt silences. "A pain, dat vun," she muttered darkly about Ethan.

As she walked slowly back to the house, squinting softly across the grazing land, a great sense of God's presence came to her so strongly that she stopped and looked around. He was not quite the same in church as He was here in the fields. In church He seemed solemn-faced like the minister she had known as a child, far off, as if He was waiting for all the prayers and hymn-singing to soften Him up. But here in the open He was a tender Father, inviting her to come and share His thoughts. He was Holy Fire, drawing her from her fear of snakes and from her self-love and self-pity. "Herre Gud," she prayed, slipping back into

Norwegian, "I have tried to be a good person, but I am seeing that this is not enough. I want to know you like John and Kip do. Please forgive me for my sin and selfishness, and make me more like Jesus—and less like Urliss. Ah, my lovely Lord, your love cradles me now, and washes me." Her breath caught in a sob.

Joy filled her, spreading through her veins like liquid fire. Gladness had danced with her before in tripping little waltzes that had made her flush with the thrill and promise of it. But now it saturated her, sweeping away the melancholy shrew crouching under the dark willows of grief and disappointment. Her spirit was healed! And suddenly she knew that the most glorious treasure to be had in all the world was hers: fellowship with the Lord Gud!

And revelation came to her now. Her spirit had found its grave in those sad, solemn days beside her dying sweetheart and broken angel boy in order that she might find a higher life. She had died inside in order to find another new birth! She was elated with this realization and increased her pace until she was almost running back to the house.

But later when Anna came to glean news of Kip, her face pinched and pale and very drawn, Urliss turned cold and unbending in spite of a persistent voice deep in her soul warning her against the old ways of thinking. She stubbornly ignored it. "John tells us he lost his legs," Anna said anxiously, as if she was begging Urliss to deny it.

"Yah," Urliss consented. "Doctor say he does as good as expected under such conditions. Soon I vill be vid him and know firsthand all dere be to know. Till den—" she shrugged and took cruel pleasure in Anna's drooping head as she turned back to the road. Urliss did not approve of this Anna having anything to do with Kip. She was out of some backwash scandal, you bet, and not good enough for her angel boy. She sighed over the too-familiar distance again separating her from her Lord but was too stubborn to give in, at least yet.

At last Urliss received word from Kip that Ethan would be returning to school after Thanksgiving so she could come and keep her vigil beside him. Excitement called little sounds from her throat as she trembled through the rest of Kip's message: My new legs are as cute as Miss America's and nearly as efficient.

(Of course the football fans will be disappointed, but they'll probably work through it.) "Poor, brave boy," Urliss murmured. Anticipation over the trip and seeing Kip helped her shrug off the feeling that she had displeased God.

She tackled her chores. Her suitcase had been packed and ready for weeks, but she gave special attention to her appearance, washing and brushing her hair until it glistened like stubble under a new sun. As she made a date cake for Kip, she reminded herself how she must not weep; she must laugh and tell funny stories. Picking her memory for a bit of humor, she discovered it all eluded her. Strain though she did, her mind had lapsed back into lonely grief.

The next day she dressed in her boots and suede jacket, crowned her head with an orange tam and set out with John on the first leg of her journey.

They chatted amiably during the first miles of their drive to the city in the big Lincoln that Dow had left to Urliss, then lapsed into a polite silence that lasted most of the way to the airport where they had allowed two hours of spare time before Urliss's flight.

After they had checked her baggage Urliss urged, "You go on now, John, get de tings you need for de ranch. Is good I am early vid time to hoof around and get de knots outta my legs." She grinned and extended her hand. When he returned her smile she saw that a little scar pressed against his mouth, making him look a little bit comical and very sad. She caught her breath. Poor John, always strong and calm. How sad he must be now. As she studied him there in the bold light of day, she suddenly caught her breath in the naked revelation of his eyes and turned away in confusion. He cares for me, she thought, and surprise came like a flower in the grass. But he will never tell me so; he does not tink himself good enough for me. She turned back to him, smiling with puzzled tenderness at his gentle, dark face. How fine he was, how kind and yet how strong. "Is good for us dat I go now, John," she said, hoping to convey a message beyond its surface meaning. "I tink about us and our tomorrows, and you, also, John? Hmm?"

John nodded and his smile grew broader, but his unassuming humility read no implications into her words. Yes, he would secure her tomorrows with hard work, his smile said. Her newly owned herds would be safe with him, and he would be here if ever she or Kip needed him.

Urliss shook his hand solemnly before turning away at last. "You take care now, John, and you get more rest, hmm?" she said kindly, "Ve be back before you know it; don't take a vooden nickel. *Farvel—adjo.*"

"I'll watch it," John assured her with a little mock salute. "Give my love to that boy of ours. I likely won't get over to see him again before they send him home; but if he needs me, you give a holler and I'll take the first train." He turned and went away in that fluid gait that had become so familiar to Urliss.

After she lost sight of the retreating John, Urliss found herself passing the time comfortably, smiling in open empathy at others who were milling around, waiting to speak their farewells or waiting to fly away. When the sun broke through the opaline sky, she squinted at it, catching sight of silver wings coming. With sudden exhilaration she broke into her long, free stride toward the ramp.

Comfortably in her seat and staring out the window at the clouds, like whipped cream below the plane, Urliss acknowledged that she had been her old, unyielding self when it came to Kip. "Dear Lord, I ask you to forgive me for my unkindness to Anna," she prayed. "And I give him to you. I tank you if you vill use me to care for him." Tears came to her eyes when she realized that she again had fellowship with her Lord.

It was mid-afternoon when John left the city, and it occurred to him that Urliss would already be approaching Seattle. The thought brought his appraisal of her in its wake: she was pure and lovely, like a snow princess, a great and good lady. In his mind he knelt before her, knowing that any real man would honor her. "Dow was worthy of her," he thought. Then he was conscious of a hurting in his chest, like a grain of stone in a mollusk, as he remembered that his companion of earlier, easier days had sealed himself off these last years and had sent him away while he lay dying.

Or maybe it was the other way around. Maybe it was John's fault that he had failed to meet Dow on ground they held common, their love for the land, their mutual respect for the qualities of integrity. "I miss seein' you around," he said aloud, softly.

Now his mind shifted to Kip, and he prayed again for him. Along with Ethan, John had accompanied Kip to the hospital in Seattle where medical experts could work on the boy's legs. John had stayed right beside him and Ethan during those first critical days. When he had come out of the dark Kip had said, "John, tell Anna to ride Dierdre sometimes."

But in the press of the work scene John had neglected to deliver the message, and he thought of it now as he approached the turn onto the county road where the commune stood out like a johnny weed in a cornfield. As he turned into the gate, he spied Brother Rich out walking and drew alongside.

Rich smiled a welcome in his kind, nearsighted way. "Well, Brother John, the air is full of farewells. It's a sad time."

"So you're breaking up. Understand part of your bunch is leaving right away."

"Yessir. Back to their homes, some to the cities where they can get work. Others are going on to Bible college."

John was moved by Rich's solemn attitude. On many occasions he had entered into the sweetness of the brothers and sisters' love and commitment to one another. Sentiment might be buried under ten layers of veneer elsewhere, but in the commune the women's faces were swollen with weeping, and the men very tender in their comfort. The plaintive wail of Bobby's harmonica came to him, reminding him of shared bread and sorrows, the naked longing in them all for family ties that spoke of caring and security.

"We've all agreed to keep only the rude necessities for ourselves, John," Rich went on, "remembering that we must spread the kingdom of God through humble service and sharing our money. We're only strangers passing through a world crying with needs."

"I know your sincerity, Rich," John said. "Are you staying on?"

"A few of us are, just through the winter. I've taken a job as janitor in the new rest home. We'll get by," he sighed. "We might've worked things better if I'd had a better grasp of the farm picture, but we just couldn't seem to keep ahead of the wolf." With brooding hindsight, he seemed to be asking for understanding.

"The prairie's a tough mistress, Rich. She can do wonders with a pinch of rain, but you gotta have the right equipment. It's sure no place for gardening."

"I've learned that much. Yessir, unless the Lord works a miracle—" he broke off.

"A lot of good has been done here, you can claim that," John assured him kindly.

Although John felt sorry for them, he was privately relieved that they were going away. He was tired of being the man in the keyhole, responsible to his church and the community for these young dreamers. This whole scheme was impractical, and he felt guilt for encouraging it scrabble around his brain like a bird trapped in the attic. "I'll miss seeing you traipsing around this forty," he said truthfully; "miss those songs carried on the wind from the potato field." He sighed, wondering whether he was a fool and a meddler like some good folks thought. Maybe he had even harmed these children more than he had helped them. "Almost forgot why I came," he said finally. "I have a message for Anna Vladmore. Where can I find her?"

"I'll get her; sit tight." Rich disappeared into the schoolhouse.

But Anna came alone in a few minutes, her face streaked with tears. "Oh, Brother John, these are the hardest good-byes I've ever made. I feel like I'm going to break in bits and pieces." She threw her apron over her face to cover a fresh bath of tears. "These were the best times most of us ever knew," she told John when she could get her voice.

"Now that you know what it is to get settled down in Christ and His love for one another, there'll be happy times for you wherever you go."

"Did you know I'm going home, John, back to Mama and Papa, to Seattle, my hometown? Gonna take the love of Jesus to my folks. Oh, John, I can't tell you how my heart aches for them. I want them to know how much they mean to me. It's really neat the way Christ gives us love for everyone, and how He moves in to heal broken relationships."

"Mighty glad to hear it," John agreed heartily. "I'm sure Ben and Rich are proud of you for accepting your responsibility to your folks."

"They are, and I know God is pleased. I've been writing to my folks for several months now—it's like we're getting to know each other."

"Well, your mentioning Seattle reminds me of why I'm here. I failed to give you a message from Kip." John did not miss how every pulse in her became hushed and listening. "He wanted me to ask if you'd ride Dierdre sometimes, but I guess I'm a little late."

Anna looked very troubled, staring around herself. "John, should I visit him?" she asked finally. "I swore I'd never see him again!"

"Well, in that case—I sure don't know what to tell you." He made a hasty move toward the car.

"Wait, please, John. Wait a minute, let me think."

"So you need me here to think?" John grinned, but he was weary and anxious to get on home.

"I'm so crazy about him, John. I love him so much. Next to Christ, he's the loveliest man ever born. But I'm not the one for him. I know it and God knows it and so does Urliss. Oh, boy, does Urliss know it!" She bowed her head and her hair parted over her long vulnerable neck. "There was someone else once."

For a long time John did not answer. "I can't help you there, Anna," he said finally. "I see you for what you are now, a pure and lovely Christian woman. But I've had enough experience with people to know that problems in our past, especially where we've dishonored ourselves or others, cling to the deep places in us. God forgives and we're fresh and new in His sight, but the barnacles in our subconscious don't just go away like magic. That's one reason why sin is so deadly."

Anna did not raise her head, and her voice, when it came, sounded muffled. "I'd die for him. I couldn't stand to have my past come up to hurt him." She looked up, misery in her face. "But John, is it just coincidence that he's in Seattle, right where I'm heading? Could it be the Lord is opening a door for us, John?"

John smiled a little, his eyes crinkling as he followed her thoughts. "Seattle just happened to have the best hospital for

Kip's needs; our local doctors did what they could and flew him on. That's all. But talk to the Lord about it. Kip needs a friend right away, but don't make him dependent on you unless you're planning to stick with it."

"Thanks, Brother John." Anna turned away. "I've got to go now; I'll see you around sometime."

"Evenin', Anna." John drove away, puzzling over his conversation with Anna until he decided to give the whole matter to the Lord. How tired he was. He looked back once at the lighted windows in the schoolhouse, and it seemed his place there was calling to him, holding out its arms to him.

But another place was calling to him. The unrelenting work at Shellydown and the additional burden now of Dow's spread was getting to be too much to both manage and work.

Other voices were calling also: the voice of his young wife from long ago, murmuring to the death angel as she gave birth to John's son; the voice of John's mother, keeping her lonely vigil by his uncle's wigwam, calling out to her son, the half-breed rejected by his white father gone back to his own kind. *Better stay on the Reservation, John Rainwater. Put in for gov'ment pension. Keep your own son on Indian land.*

But John had to find the last country spared from iron birds and sick fish, land of sky and wind and sun, shunned by big bellies and soft limbs, land where the ghosts of the Indian nation went slinking around their campfires still, raising their chants to the moon like a sleeper's bedtime song.

"So I came to the prairie," John explained now to the memories, "only to find that she had hung up her flute and yielded her virginity to the marketplace. But there was He, the white man's God, haunting the land."

He looked at me, and I looked at Him, lonely together. And He wooed me over the hollows of His blue-eyed braves gone away to dance in their black slick.

I see you, Great Spirit, I see you, Father God, I see you, Master Christ. Together we will roam this land, and I will learn your ways and win back your children to you.

When John pulled into the garage with the big car a coyote howled far off, the lonely lament stalking his innards. Slowly he got out and pulled down the garage door and stood for a moment, looking up at the pale moon sandwiched between frail clouds that made it look like a gleaming cup. "I'm lonesome for you, Master Christ," he whispered. "I'm feeling that homing instinct down deep inside."

Suddenly he froze in his tracks and listened. The dogs must be out chasing, he thought, putting down a sudden uneasiness. The night was moving in on him and his breath made steam on the air. It smelled like snow. He was striking out for the bunkhouse when suddenly his flesh started crawling. Something was wrong. Even as he detected a movement from the shadow of the front porch, four men moved out into full view under the pale moon. "Hey there," one of them called, "you Johnson?"

"Yessir," John watched them approach warily, sensing the spirit in them, dark and menacing.

"Yeah, well, we're buddies of Tig Gleason down at your forty acres. Know 'im?"

John hesitated. " 'Fraid not," he said.

"No difference. We hear you help folks in need. That's white of you. We need a little help ourselves. Maybe we could interest ya in a little deal."

"Maybe." Slowly John reached for his wallet and handed it to the one who was doing the talking. "Help yourself," he said softly.

"Now this ain't near enough," the malefactor said, rifling through the wallet compartments and pocketing the twenty-dollar bill and odd change. "Not near enough, dad." At that moment the dusk called the yardlight into play, and John saw the faces of these hoodlums, vile and animal-like. "Yeah, we need a lot more bucks than this and some wheels and anything else you wanta spare."

"Take anything you want; I don't have any more cash."

"Hey, you're puttin' us on, aintcha?" He started to hoot and cackle and the others joined him, all of them laughing as if they were sharing a great joke.

Revulsion skidded through John's stomach like a slivered board. They're devils, he thought, on hard drugs, and they want some fun with me. "You can have anything I've got, my saddle is worth something, anything else you want, but I need time to get cash."

They broke into a fresh fit of laughter, bending over themselves until they seemed to lose interest. And then they moved in on John, beating him to the ground and standing over him like vultures. "We'll give you two minutes to tell us where your wad is."

"I'm a man of peace," John gasped, struggling to get up, "why would you want to hurt me? God loves us all. . . ." But they kicked him back flat to the ground, each one keeping one booted foot resting easily on his body.

Silence now as the clouds floated over the cup-shaped moon.

The first sound was the tapping of three drops of sleet on the garage roof—ta, ta, ta.

Suddenly with wild grunts and whoops, they flailed at him, picking him up and battering him about like a large rag doll.

After they had done their worst with their boots and fists, John returned from some remote cavern to catch a glimpse of knife blades flashing through blurred and wet vision. His assailants were preparing for some vile finale to their unspeakable deed.

And John saw something else—indistinct but definite. The Enemy, the author of violence and evil, was here in these tormented gangsters, trying to destroy him. John thought he heard the enemy's voice, harsh against his face, "You figured He'd save you, didn't you?" he jeered.

John's answer made gurgling sounds in his throat. "It matters not to me, Satan, whether I am butchered for His sake or die in my sick bed someday. His truth will go on. His victory will come. The glory of the Lord will cover the earth, from shore to shore.

"His is a greater power than yours, Satan. Jesus Christ has power over you and all your works of darkness. All power in heaven and in earth is His. There is power in His name! The Name that makes your demons tremble and shake. He is here in my broken body and all around me! Jesus, Jesus!"

At the sound of John's call to Christ, one of the assailants was so terrified that he threw down his knife and fled. Another, whimpering like a frightened dog, followed. And then the last two, with gutteral cursing, chased after their companions.

For a long time John lay still, his broken body oozing with blood and saturated with an ecstatic humility. He praised God with tears streaming. With slow and agonizing movements, he crawled to the house and called for the Ordlow ambulance.

14

Ariel from the Prairie

Cum, Sanctu Spiritu!
Thread our tongues with praise!
Break our hearts with pity,
Shame us with the fruits
of our pride
Till we are Christ's light. . . .

IN HIS DREAMS Kip had remembered the great cloudburst when his life hung between it and the fire, and in his conscious moments he knew that Ethan was never far from him. Lights came at him, blue and dark pink and sharp white and faces hung over him like pears and tambourines full of eyes, sad even when crinkled with smiles, and there were voices falling down on him like waters over a cliff.

Sometimes he could tell what the voices were saying: "Let's turn this way, shall we? There's a brave, good fellow . . . good-looking boy, beautiful face, beautiful. . . ."

And he knew that his legs felt strange, with bugs skittering up and down them and into his feet.

And he kept trying to define the reason for his being so sad and lonely and wanting to die. (Maybe it was because Ethan would be going away to get married and they would never be together in the same way again.) But he kept saying, over and over, "Jesus, come and get me. Take me to heaven. Mama and Daddy, I'm coming home; I'm all done here."

And then one day it all came together, the colored lights became yellow and the tambourine face with the sad, crinkling eyes said to him, "Your brother is here, say hello." And in a little while he felt the bugs crawling in his legs again, clear down to his toes, and he looked down at them and saw that there were casts from his hips down to his knees but no further. There were no more legs. The doctor said, "Son, we're all in this with you. It's not the end. We'll give you new limbs which will make your getting around pretty decent; think of what President Roosevelt did with his handicap."

But after Ethan had gone back to his motel that night, Kip fell down into an abyss that sucked him at high speed into a cold, black vacuum where there was no sound at all and no bottom. Desperately he looked for the end. There he was sure he could get rid of the feeling of his heart weeping blood.

He did not rave against God that night even though He had left him in a hellfire, bramble bed. His heart finally gave out like a melting snowball, falling away into the black, bloody wet that ran into his hellfire bramble bed, until he could feel no difference between his heart and his body, both of them gone away to numb nothingness.

But finally a winged bird tapped against the window of his soul and he voiced his rage against God.

"You hate me!" he accused. "Why didn't you show me as much mercy as a wild animal and let me die! I trusted you, trusted you! You didn't deserve my trust! You betrayed me!" His mind reeled under the bitter sorrow of one who expected preferential treatment and had received, instead, open shame.

"What did you have against me?" he demanded clear into the night. "Didn't I tell Ethan I had the joy and wouldn't trade it for all the world? Didn't I boast how you took care of your own children?"

But when he was spent with raging and spewing and lay helpless and forlorn as a babe in a thicket, the Holy Spirit came all around him, like a mother cradling him in her arms and crooning comforts that he could not hear but felt deep in his soul so that all he could do was bawl and cry. This happened night after night, until finally, in the midst of his tears, a little bright light, no bigger than a bead, broke through the window where the bird tapped yet, and Kip grew still.

That night he had a dream, so vivid and real that he awoke with the knowledge that the dream was reality.

In the dream Christ had spoken to Kip. "My son," he had

said, love pouring through his voice, "I am bearing this with you. I am in the center of your grief. You must trust me and love me with praise for the healing of your broken spirit. Then I will make you a chosen vessel for a work that requires much compassion and patience."

Kip awakened that morning with such a sense of joy that a new awareness of spiritual infilling—which had lifted him to a world of pearls all running together in shimmering, white light—was giving him an impersonal view of his life as a preparation for ministries, both temporal and eternal.

And it gave him a fresh touch of Christ and a consuming passion for Him so that he became quiet and yielded before Him, no longer agonizing with his poor, legless body.

From where he lay on his back, he filled empty hours with praise and adoration to the Father, and he felt his soul being lifted to the highest heaven.

Once more the Holy Spirit called to him through a dream. This time Kip clearly saw the children of America lost in a vast, gnarled jungle, groping pitifully through its yawning tendrils while evil captors lurked in the shadows, waiting with cages and chains to make them slaves. Some of the children were so terrified, they were trying to kill themselves. Their desolation gave agony to Kip so that he screamed into his head and raced across the prairie with the bugs skittering up and down his legs, empathy clinging to his innards.

And then he remembered the Holy Father, whose great heart was broken for the lost children, and he called out to Him. "Help them, Father, show them the way to safety! Oh, save them. You cannot stand it, you cannot!"

And then, with total clarity, Kip had known what he was to do.

When Urliss had arrived in Seattle, rain and wind were chasing old leaves through the streets, making all the trees shake and dance. The sun peeped nervously through the storm, though, and the momentum of city life excited her. "How good be all de traffic," she cried, within the privacy of her motel. "How be-yootiful all de people!" She spent only minutes refreshing herself before taking a shuttle bus to the hospital where Kip was waiting.

"Hello," she trilled as she came swiftly into his room, scattering nurses and gloom, exercising the greatest self-control to gaze nowhere except on Kip's face.

"Hello yourself," he replied with smiles and chuckles. "Never so glad to see anyone in my whole life," Kip said as she hugged him and drew up a chair.

"I cannot speak, I cannot," she said, holding his hand gently and watching his expression with soft, shining eyes. "Kip, you are glowing vid light!" she exclaimed. "I come to pity, but already you have took it!"

"So why not? I'm walking, Urliss! Wait'll you see me strut down the corridor. Next week I'll have my permanent legs, and it'll blow you away to see what a job they do. They're attached by suction and they look for all the world like my own legs. And they tell me I won't scare little kids and old ladies when they see me coming. Right now I lear around like one of Doctor Schindler's robots."

"You can valk every place?" Urliss was thrilled with the prospect of even limited mobility.

"Walk, ski, ride old Dierdre. I'll do it all, you'll see." He looked at her intently. "But the greatest thing happening is in my spirit, Urliss. I've had a fresh meeting with Christ. He's so real, Urliss, so close to me. His presence is so powerful and we're sharing something very special." Near tears, he opened his hands and grinned. "Hey, this is a great place, best staff in the country. They make me right at home!"

Urliss continued to beam and nod, listening respectfully. "How good and vise you be, Kip. How qvick you lay your childhood to rest. Now you have gone beyond your years," she shook her head. "You are a great varrior," she added, enunciating each word carefully. "John say you be a prince. Yah, a varrior prince."

"You wouldn't've thought so the first week around here. I howled like a baby. And I can't take credit for my change of attitude, Urliss. Do you know that was entirely the work of the Lord?" He broke off pensively. "Amazing, amazing."

"Someting dere for Him to vork vid," she insisted.

Through all the days that followed, Urliss carefully did what she could for Kip, watching him closely. His gentle mouth creased only now and then with pain, as the gold flecks in his eyes changed to smoldering blue and back again. And never did it occur to her that she was repeating the grim posture of those months with Dow; she had caught the light of Kip's soul and had been prepared through suffering to receive it.

His laborious movements with his false legs made her cry with joy. "Vonderful!" she exclaimed over and over as he made his way down the hall and back. "Each time is better!"

"I don't want to be a burden to you, Urliss," he said when they were resettled in his room once more.

"You! A burden? Never! Someday, ven you marry, den I go avay."

"Not far, I hope," he said, a sort of wistful sadness coming to play.

Urliss was pleased. "Not far—I hope," she agreed.

Ethan kept the telephone busy for a while every day. Today Ethan told Kip that he and Melanie were investigating the claims of Christ through Campus Crusade and through some of the writings of Tozer and Lewis. "But I have to admit," Ethan hurried on, "that you're my favorite chessman, little brother; I want to follow you down the road."

Kip was so moved he could not struggle through his tears to speak, so he handed the phone to Urliss, who gave Ethan the business while Kip blew his nose. "Who you tink you be, calling here to hurt your bruder who has been trough hell and all over? Such a toughtless—"

"Urliss, for Pete's sake!"

Kip suddenly recovered and grabbed back the phone. "Hey, Ethan," he cried.

"—cracks me up," Ethan was saying; "she's funnier than a Charlie Chaplin movie."

"Yeah, I know," Kip agreed sheepishly. "Hey, you just gave me the best piece of news I ever had!

"Ethan, you're ripe for the picking, you and Melanie. There's no way you can escape from finding the real life now. Jesus is the life, man. We're dead, really dead till He gets a hold of us. I'd like to pray for you right now if I could, right here on the phone."

"Well, sure, little brother, say your prayers."

"Lord," Kip prayed, "next to knowing you the greatest thing I can think of is for Ethan and Melanie to know you also. He's a plum ripe for the picking, Lord, and I'm claiming the fruit right now. Please save him and sanctify him and fill him and use him for your glory; and don't forget Melanie. Thank you, Jesus. Amen."

Ethan was silent for a minute. "Wow," he said finally. "You're right. I do need that and so does Melanie."

"Well, there's no better time than now to start," Kip continued.

Kip listened, awestruck as Ethan agreed and began falteringly to pray on the other end of the line. His joy was ready to explode by the time Ethan finished.

"Ethan, I love you," he almost shouted. "Now we're brothers two times over. Go talk to someone on campus right now, and tell 'em what's happened."

"Yeah, I think I'd like to do that."

"You'll be okay," Kip assured him.

"Melanie says she wants to make a commitment to Jesus, too. So we'll pray together and then go," Ethan said, signing off with an abrupt, "good-bye, we'll talk later."

"Think of it, Urliss—Ethan and Melanie." Once more he struggled with his feelings. "We'll have to swim out of here if I don't get a hold of myself."

Urliss was knitting. "So. Dey've found Christ, too. I hope ve get along better now."

"Listen, Urliss, I had a dream one night that put me right out in space. As a result of that dream, I gave everything I am and have, every blade of grass, every dollar, to God. And He gave me the word on what He wants to do with it.

"Urliss, we need a place for some of the messed-up runaway kids in this country. It's still in the vision stage, and it'll take more practical sense that I can muster at the moment to bring it all together, but as sure as I'm lying here it's going to happen. We can do it, you and John and maybe Ben and Rich and me—and God. We're enough to start. Ethan's conversion makes it a lead-pipe cinch!"

Urliss gazed at him solemnly. "You mean to care for children like at de commune?"

"Yep, only I'd want it to be a real home, a place where kids can find a family. We'll have a ranch that offers freedom with responsibility, a home that offers Christ and love."

Urliss started knitting faster. No good telling him that she had little patience for the rebellious, forlorn kids he was talking about, or that she would like a normal life with children of her own. "Vell, if I be dere dey go to church and no nonsense!" she warned.

"You bet!"

"Dey mind or down de road dey go!"

"There'll be the right kind of discipline," Kip agreed.

"Vell, ve see," she consented slowly. "I vill have rules," she said firmly.

Kip looked deep into her soul. "Do I have the right to ask you to help, Urliss? I know it's selfish, but what could any of us do without you now?"

"Is very good qvestion," she said evenly.

"How old are you, Urliss?"

"Almost tirty-six," she said quietly.

Kip thought about that. "You don't look that old, not by a long shot." Later he added, "God made the sun stand still for Joshua. Maybe He'll keep you right at thirty-five till the captain of your ship comes by for you and sweeps you off to your ocean cruiser."

Tears welled up as the maiden in her called out once more for her dancing slippers, drawing aside the dark mantilla of her old mournings for just a moment before she closed it tightly and gave herself to the Lord's calling to help this boy realize his dream.

"I respect you so much, Urliss. You're everything a real woman should be. If I were twenty years older, no sea captain'd ever have a chance." He smiled as her chin trembled with the colony of dimples twisted with the torrent of her stopped-up feelings.

"Tank you, Kip," she said humbly. "Ve bot be very tired; I go now, back to my motel. You behave tonight." She pressed his hand and went swiftly away.

She had just settled into her bath when the phone rang, and Ethan had to tell her the news that John had been beaten within an inch of his life by some young hoodlums just a few yards from the bunkhouse. "He's out of the woods now, but he'll be in the hospital for a long time. Urliss, those four punks were plumb crazy. They killed Pliny and Albert—before John ever came home."

Urliss gasped. "Ah, Etan, so sorry I am. How cruel and despising!"

"Well, some good has come out of it, I guess. At least John thinks so. The fanatics are going to John's church. They've decided to come out of their shell and take a different attitude about cooperation. Seems they feel responsible about blazing a trail for off-beat characters to follow, although it's anybody's guess as to whether the kooks who hit had a bead on the commune."

"You very sure John vill be okay?" Part of her was stunned, and she could not seem to get her thoughts together.

"He's too tough and stubborn to keep down for long. But I'm looking for some good hands to replace him. Ben Rutledge offered to help; nice guy." He sighed deeply. "I'd better go, Urliss. Now don't worry about a thing, and don't say a word to Kip about this yet. I felt you should know about John. Write him a get-well note. He admires you a lot. It'll cheer him up."

Afterward Urliss sat on the edge of her bed and stared at the wall for a long time. "Herre Gud, vat is de vorld coming to? Poor, dear John," she whispered over and over. A sudden and urgent longing to see him made her agitated. How could she leave Kip? She could not, no, she could not. "Ah, Lord, show me vat to do," she pleaded.

Through the night she peered dry-eyed into the dark. "Must be a hex on me," she decided; "all my men hounded by tragedy." The thought drew sighs from her—long, weary expulsions of air that did not relieve the heaviness of her heart.

Finally she got out of bed and knelt down and released her feelings through a torrent of tears and native tongue, at last accepting the idea that she had been called to that remote spot in the prairie to bring comfort to the lives of those broken ones. It was then that peace came over her like a soft glove and she fell asleep.

It was nearly noon when she awakened to spats of rain tapping at the window, calling her to the gray, sad world of responsibility.

Reproaching herself for the lateness of the hour when she walked into Kip's hospital room, she stopped short at the sight of Anna Vladmore seated beside him, chirping at him like a little bird. Now vat is dis? Urliss wondered under her breath. Vat goes here? While her former troubled responses pounded against her mind, another part of her was calm and unruffled, listening to a wisdom which she could not yet put into words.

"Ah, Anna, vat a surprise you be." Her recognition of Anna was, for the first time, genuinely warm and friendly. Whatever Anna might have been back there in the winter of her transgression, the Spirit of Christ was in her now and her devotion to Kip was there in her eyes, Urliss decided, drawing up a chair to a position slightly behind Anna. She reached out and patted Kip on his fingers. "You look bright-eye and bushy-tail," she said, smiling.

Their eyes met and locked. "Anna's here, Urliss," he said huskily. "My two favorite women have just made it all come together."

Still smiling, Urliss said, "How long she can stay?" addressing her question to Kip.

Anna ducked her head shyly. "This is my home town, you know. I've moved back."

Urliss thought about that. "Dat so. Vell, good, good. I s'pose you vill be back sometime to see Kip again."

She smiled nervously. "Every day, if you'd want," she said softly.

"Is up to Kip," Urliss replied, matter-of-factly.

"Then she'll come every day," he said, smiling at Anna before turning to look fully at Urliss.

"So, vill you?" Urliss asked Anna with careful interest.

She shook her head meekly. "Of course—if you don't mind."

"I do not mind," Urliss said. "In fact, if dat be a promise, I must go back to de ranch a veek or so."

Kip said, "Something wrong, Urliss?"

She shrugged and patted his hand. She had agreed with Ethan to withhold news of John's beating from Kip. "John may need me; he is alone now, you know."

Kip fell to studying her. Finally he smiled. "So John might need you, eh? Well, in that case we'll let you off for a day or two, hmm, Anna?"

"Last night Etan call me at motel. You vill be glad to know your friends are gone into John's church," Urliss said to Anna, a note of triumph in her voice. "He say de commune must try to hold togeder dis vinter; dey have jobs now and go to church. Vat you tink?"

"Hey, that's great!" Kip said, giving Anna time to mull over the news.

"So, Kip has won his battle," Anna mused. "He's lectured us now and then on working for church renewal from within. I think this proves you're right, Kip," she added. "If we want to lift the world up to Christ, we'd better work together."

"See there, she's catching on fast. Listen, Urliss, I just finished telling Anna about our plans for the ranch, and she's as excited as we are."

Urliss looked puzzled for a moment, and then her face cleared. "So it is all come togeder," she said, partly addressing God as she looked through Him to all the persons and events that He appeared to be bringing together for His purpose. "He is Almighty Gud," she said, shaking her head with feeling, "a tender, loving Fader to us all. Kip, I have come to love Christ vid great power. I love you, also, and John and Etan. And Anna," she added, moved even further by the wonder of it. "Yah, I love you all, and ve do His vill, come flood or dustpan."

"His will is everything," Kip agreed, his own eyes wet with emotion. "I can say from my bed, I'm learning to love His will, to want it with all my heart." Reaching out to both of them, he said, "Give me your hand, Urliss, and Anna, too."

The three of them joined hands, their eyes shut against everything except the inner light whose presence filled the room, covering them with benediction.

A nurse came into the room, her gaze going to the strong, legless boy and the golden lady and the dark-haired girl. They were holding hands, their eyes closed; they were smiling. And there was something about them, a shining brightness, that made her stop and catch herself and look around as if she expected to see someone else in the room.

But of course there was no one else. A sense of yearning gripped her. What is it, she mused, what is this anyway? Suddenly it came to her that she was the observer of a holy joy but not a participant. She was sensing a spirit she could not enter into.

Yes, yes, she would talk to them later, the nurse decided with a feeling of urgency as she slipped away. She would corner them and insist that they tell her how she might find the presence, that exquisite, indefinable Someone who was theirs.

"Where is He?" she would ask them. "I want Him, too. Tell me now, where will I find Him?"

CHRISTIAN HERALD ASSOCIATION AND ITS MINISTRIES

CHRISTIAN HERALD ASSOCIATION, founded in 1878, publishes The Christian Herald Magazine, one of the leading interdenominational religious monthlies in America. Through its wide circulation, it brings inspiring articles and the latest news of religious developments to many families. From the magazine's pages came the initiative for CHRISTIAN HERALD CHILDREN'S HOME and THE BOWERY MISSION, two individually supported not-for-profit corporations.

CHRISTIAN HERALD CHILDREN'S HOME, established in 1894, is the name for a unique and dynamic ministry to disadvantaged children, offering hope and opportunities which would not otherwise be available for reasons of poverty and neglect. The goal is to develop each child's potential and to demonstrate Christian compassion and understanding to children in need.

Mont Lawn is a permanent camp located in Bushkill, Pennsylvania. It is the focal point of a ministry which provides a healthful "vacation with a purpose" to children who without it would be confined to the streets of the city. Up to 1000 children between the ages of 7 and 11 come to Mont Lawn each year.

Christian Herald Children's Home maintains year-round contact with children by means of an *In-City Youth Ministry*. Central to its philosophy is the belief that only through sustained relationships and demonstrated concern can individual lives be truly enriched. Special emphasis is on individual guidance, spiritual and family counseling and tutoring. This follow-up ministry to inner-city children culminates for many in financial assistance toward higher education and career counseling.

THE BOWERY MISSION, located at 227 Bowery, New York City, has since 1879 been reaching out to the lost men on the Bowery, offering them what could be their last chance to rebuild their lives. Every man is fed, clothed and ministered to. Countless numbers have entered the 90-day residential rehabilitation program at the Bowery Mission. A concentrated ministry of counseling, medical care, nutrition therapy, Bible study and Gospel services awakens a man to spiritual renewal within himself.

These ministries are supported solely by the voluntary contributions of individuals and by legacies and bequests. Contributions are tax deductible. Checks should be made out either to CHRISTIAN HERALD CHILDREN'S HOME or to THE BOWERY MISSION.

Administrative Office: 40 Overlook Drive, Chappaqua, New York 10514
Telephone: (914) 769-9000